OFF THE DEEP END

EMILY SILVER

TRAVELIN' HOOSIER BOOKS

Chapter One

WES

"All clear."

"All clear?" I parrot back, staring at the doctor from my spot on the table. It's been months of appointments, sitting here, listening to him tell me that it'll only be a few more weeks. Now, that day is finally here.

"You're good to start training." Dr. Abrams, an older man with salt-and-pepper hair, claps me on the shoulder.

"Practice, training, competitions? Everything?"

"Everything. You've put in the work in rehab, now it's time for you to train." He smiles back at me. "This is good news, Wes."

"Yeah, right. It's just hard to believe."

I scrub a hand through the stubble on my jaw. It's been months since that fateful day. When I landed funny during training and ruptured my Achilles, I thought my career was over. But it's been a strenuous path back here to get where I am now—sitting on the table in my doctor's office hearing those beautiful words.

"If you ever need anything, you know where to find me."

"Thanks, doc." I shake his hand, hopping off the table.

"Just remember me when you win gold."

I laugh, turning to leave his office. The receptionist waves as I pull the door open, walking out into the bright, Northern California day. I twist around, looking at the tendon that's been causing me so much grief lately. No one would know, the scar from surgery barely noticeable now.

One wrong landing and my entire world almost came crumbling down on top of me. I let out a deep breath I didn't realize I was holding.

My entire life is diving. But these last few months have been nothing but rehab, working to regain strength in my left leg. And now it seems like the world is in front of me. And what a scary feeling that is.

"YOU GOT CLEARED? That's fucking fantastic!" Damien swallows me in a hug. He's been my coach since I tanked at the last Olympics. The first stop I made after the doctor was the NorCal Aquatic Center. It's been a few weeks since I was last here. Walking in the door, smelling the chlorine, was too hard before. To see everyone diving and doing what I love made sitting on the sidelines that much harder.

"I'm ready to train. I'm ready to get back out there." Nervous energy has been flowing through me since I left the doctor. For the last four months, really. Try telling an elite athlete who is always on the go that they have to sit still and rest.

"Relax, Wes. We still have plenty of time to get you back into shape before the first qualifiers. We don't want you hurting yourself because you went balls to the wall your first day back."

I roll my eyes at him. "They've only gone over this in rehab about a million times, D. I know what I need to do."

His blue eyes pierce mine with a serious stare. "I mean it, Wes. I don't want you overdoing it. One freak accident was hard enough to overcome, but another that we could have prevented? I'll kill you myself."

"When's the first competition?" I lean against the wall in Damien's small office.

"January. We'll have some training camps in the next few months. Will you be ready by then?"

Six months. I've trained harder in shorter periods of time. After my dismal performance at the last Olympics, I've been pushing myself to be ready for next summer. It's been my sole focus for the last three years.

"Yes." My voice is firm. "With you by my side, what could possibly go wrong?"

Damien raps on the desk with his knuckles. "Don't jinx it!"

"You're too superstitious," I say on a laugh.

"Well, you're probably not going to like me too much when I tell you what I've got planned."

"What do you have planned?" My arms drop to my sides as I move to the chair in front of his desk.

"With you being out of the spotlight for so long, I was thinking we'd do a human interest piece on you."

"Human interest piece?" I quirk a brow at him.

"A buddy of mine from college runs the *Berkeley Tribune*. We were talking the other night, and we both think it'd help drum up some good press for you ahead of the qualifiers."

"Why the fuck do I need good press?" It's not like I'm a playboy, fucking anything with two legs. People are interested in me for two weeks, every four years, then I fade into the background. Honestly, it's how I like it.

"People love a comeback story. We want to give them something to cheer for. Our hometown kid going to the Olympics and winning gold this time." Excitement drips from every word Damien is telling me.

"You know this isn't why I compete." My palms are getting sweaty.

"I know that. But you'd also be doing me a huge favor." The excitement turns to pleading.

"You mean besides trying to win you a medal?" I quirk a brow at him.

"The paper is struggling. Every two-bit chump out there who fancies themself a writer thinks they can do it. So you'd really be helping me out."

"Are you fucking him?" It's crasser sounding than I intended it to be.

"Right now? No. Back in college? Yes."

"Really, Damien?" Damien is everyone's type, man or woman. I had the biggest crush on him when I first started working with him. Blond hair, blue eyes, six-pack for days. But then he put me through my first workout, and I wanted to kill him. Nothing like feeling every bone in your body turn to liquid to kill the crush.

"Not only will this help them, but it'll help you as well. The games are a year away, and maybe it'll push you to work harder."

"Weren't you just telling me to ease back into it?"

"Do this for me. I promise, you won't regret it."

I groan, knowing I can't say no to Damien. "Why do I feel like I'm going to regret this?"

Chapter Two

FINN

"Oh, you are just wonderful. Thank you so much for helping me." The sweet old woman pats my cheek. It takes everything I have to hold back my wince.

"I'm just glad you were able to get your cat back safe and sound." She's ignoring me now, petting the gray fur of the tiny animal in her arms.

I back away from her front door, leaving her and her cat. I've been on the community beat for the last month. My editor at the *Berkeley Tribune* asked me to cover it. Demanded was more like it. It's hard to say no when your editor keeps promising you bigger and better. But so far, it's been a lot of stories about those helping the community.

Like the teenager who goes around helping people find lost pets. It's nice. I'm not jaded enough to think it's not. But it's not changing the world. When I graduated from journalism school, I wanted to write pieces that would change the world. Sure, it changed this woman's world. But it's not my end goal.

I walk the short distance back to my office. It's a tiny, dilapidated building in an older part of town. The paper I work for is small. There's not a lot of money in it, but I want it to be a stepping-stone.

Pushing through the frosted-glass door, I'm immediately summoned by my editor. "Finn. My office, now."

Knowing it's likely nothing good, I drop my messenger bag at my desk and head toward his cramped office.

"What's going on, Harry?"

"Take a seat." He points to the chair across from his desk, one that is barely visible under the piles of papers overwhelming it.

Nerves bubble in my stomach as I wait for Harry to tell me why he called me in here. I adjust my black-framed glasses, never being one to handle being called to the boss's office well.

"I have a new assignment for you."

"But you just put me on the community beat." I shift in my seat. "Am I not doing well?"

Harry waves me off. "Nothing like that. This is more long-term, and you're the only one who has some flexibility with their schedule."

"Okay. What's the assignment?"

Harry leans back in his chair, his dark brown hair falling into his eyes. "Have you heard of Wes Cooper?"

Racking my brain, it comes up completely blank. "Can't say that I have."

He tosses a stack of photos at me, and I grab them before they hit the floor. Images of a built athlete assault my eyes. "He's on the NorCal Dive Team. Cooper is returning from an injury, and his coach wants us to document his journey back."

"But I've never watched a diving event in my life." The words blurt out before I can stop them. Reporting is all I have ever wanted to do. Write stories that mean something to someone. I just graduated last year; I know I have to put in the work. And I hate when I acknowledge what limited experience I have.

"Doesn't matter. Most people probably won't know scuba diving from Olympic diving. This will be more of a human interest piece."

"And what kind of 'human interest' articles would you like me to be writing?" I flip through the pictures. Whoever this Wes Cooper is, he's attractive. There's no doubt about it.

Harry scrubs his hand over his jaw. "That's for you to figure out. You'll be following him around. Going to training, traveling with the team. I'm sure you'll come up with something."

"And what about my current assignment?"

"Do you really want to go back to writing stories about cats up in trees?"

"No!" I squeak out. I know I have to pay my dues, but I can't take another article about a pet stuck somewhere they shouldn't be.

"Good. You start tomorrow. Here's the info you need." He tosses a pad of paper my way, effectively dismissing me from his office.

***

"A DIVER? But you don't know the first thing about sports." My sister's voice is full of doubt as she stares over my shoulder. "Why would they give it to you?"

"Something about my schedule having the most flexibility." Melissa hovers over my shoulder, looking at the videos I've been watching.

"But you don't do sports." She peers over her wineglass at me, giving me a skeptical look.

"Thanks for the vote of confidence." I go back to the

laptop, trying to gain any drop of knowledge about a sport I know nothing about.

"Sorry. I'm sure this will be the assignment that puts you on the map."

"I can hear the sarcasm."

I moved in with my older sister to save money, and it's times like this that make me question that decision. Even though I have my own space in the pool house out back, whenever my niece is with her dad, Melissa wandering out to pester me makes me want my own place.

"No, I mean it," Melissa says. "They hired you for a reason. You are a talented writer. It's just being wasted right now."

"No one starts out with the hard-hitting news. I'm twenty-three. There's still plenty of time."

"I just don't want you squandering your time away in my guest house for the rest of your life."

Closing my laptop, I grab my own glass of wine. "Thank you for the bleak assessment of my life."

Moving in with my sister wasn't my first plan after college. But I couldn't deny that my measly salary wouldn't afford me an apartment in a good part of town. And saving every penny has been a benefit I didn't count on.

"Like I have room to talk. I'm a single mom with an ex who is dating a bimbo who thinks it's okay to tell my eight-year-old that she should aspire to be a supermodel."

I about drop my glass. "Are you for real?"

Melissa gulps down the rest of her wine. "Yup. This is what I have to deal with."

"You have it much worse than I do."

"I'll deal with it. But how are you going to deal?"

"What do you mean?" My brows furrow as I turn to face her.

"You're going to be writing on this guy?" She holds up

the photo of Wes flashing a megawatt smile after winning an event.

"Yeah, so?" I shrug, playing off the fact that I have been staring at it for the last hour. He has so many abs, I lost track of counting, something I could only ever dream about.

"I can see the drool from here. Those eyes and that set of abs? You'll be in love before you even meet him."

Chapter Three

FINN

I don't remember the last time I was so nervous for my first day. Even though this technically isn't my first day, I'm still anxious. Because this assignment is big. And it has the potential to lead to other assignments just like it.

Standing inside the aquatic center lobby, I breathe in a lungful of chlorinated air, feeling it sting my nose. It's going to be something I have to get used to these next few months.

Not knowing where exactly I need to go, I hitch my bag higher on my shoulder and push through the double doors. Splashing and screams echo around the cavernous area. Diving boards higher than I've ever seen make up one wall, while lap pools stretch out in front of me. The early afternoon sun is hidden through dark windows.

"You look lost." Spinning on my heel, I find an older man with blond hair and bright blue eyes.

"Hi. I'm Finn Anderson. I'm here for the story on Wes Cooper." I extend my hand out, waiting for the man to grab it.

"You're Finn?" He takes my hand in his, eyeing me up

and down. "I figured Harry would've sent me someone a little more seasoned."

I bristle at his words. "Just because I'm young doesn't mean I won't do a good job."

"I didn't mean to offend you." He throws his hands up in defense. "Harry knows what he's doing. I just don't know how Wes will react to you."

"Well, I'm here to do my job. Hopefully Wes will make it easier on me to do."

"If he's not, tell me. He can be a prickly bastard. He's doing some dives this morning from the lower heights if you want to watch before meeting him."

"Sounds good." I give the commanding man a small smile as he waves me on to follow him.

"You can watch here, and I'll make sure Wes introduces himself after practice."

"Thank you." Sitting on one of the cool bleacher seats, I take out my pen and notepad, trying to get a sense of what is going on.

I don't have one single athletic bone in my body. I run on occasion, but this is a foreign world to me. I did some research, but I still have no idea what to expect.

Divers are coming and going, performing complicated moves as they propel themselves into the water. My heart stutters in my chest more than once when they throw themselves off the ten-meter platform. The concrete structure is unforgiving as they leap off it and into the water.

I watch as people come and go. Synchronized teams are performing on the lower boards, and it's mesmerizing how they move and instinctively know what the other person is doing. I've seen videos, but it doesn't compare to seeing it live.

As the divers continue practicing, the air in the

building shifts. Someone enters the pool deck, and a round of cheers goes up. I don't need anyone to tell me who it is.

It's Wes.

Everyone is clapping him on the shoulder, hugging him, as he makes his way to the boards. They're treating him like a hero returning from battle. He exchanges some words with his coach before getting on one of the lower springboards.

I sit up straighter, taking notice of the way he carries himself. Even from a distance, I can see he's strong. Broad shoulders and thick thighs carry him down the narrow piece of aluminum.

Wes is perched at the end of the board, his eyes roving to everything around him. For a moment, they flicker over me. For that one moment, it feels like we are the only two people here. My stomach does its own dive and flips as he launches himself off the board.

Even I can tell it's a simple move. He folds himself in half in midair before extending his arms over his head and letting the water swallow him up. Cheers and whoops go up around the deck as Wes gets out of the pool directly in front of me.

Everything moves in slow motion, and time seems to stop. The man getting out of the pool is no man. He's a god, sculpted out of marble. Water sluices over his perfectly carved pecs, through the countless abs adorning his stomach. His bulging biceps flex as he runs a hand through his dark brown hair, pushing it from his face.

It's like my very own *Baywatch* moment. A smirk plays on his handsome lips, and I know I've been caught staring. I should look away, but I can't. I can't force my eyes away from this man who has now turned his back to me.

"I see you know who Wes is." A woman in a swimsuit plops down on the metal seat next to me.

"Uhh." I clear my throat, drier than the Sahara. "Yes."

"Don't worry. He seems to have that effect on most people." She gives me a bright smile, her blonde hair dripping wet around her shoulders. "I'm Simone."

"Finn."

A look of understanding passes over her face. "The reporter."

I drag a finger under my collar, pulling it farther from my neck. It's getting hot in here. "Does everyone know who I am?"

She nods. "We were told to show you the ropes. Just in case Wes is a bit growly toward you." She bumps her shoulder with mine.

"Why does everyone keep warning me about him?"

Simone only shakes her head. "Do you want to go meet him?"

I look back toward the boards, seeing Wes talking with his coach. "I don't want to interrupt him."

"You're not. Training is all day, as you'll soon learn. Better to rip the Band-Aid off now."

"Okay, sure." I pack everything away in my bag, leaving it where it lies, and follow Simone. Each step gets heavier and heavier the closer we get to where Wes is standing. It's like a lead weight has settled in my stomach, a stomach twisted into a ball of nerves at meeting the subject I'm following around these next however many months.

"Hey, Wes. I want you to meet someone." Simone's voice is sure, confident. I swallow, trying anything to coat my dry throat. I can't remember a time in my life when I've been more nervous. Being this close to a sexy man always turns me into a bumbling idiot.

Taking a step forward, my shoes slide on the pool deck, and I almost go crashing into the pool.

"Usually we wait until the second day to hit the

water." Deep brown eyes meet mine as I try to steady myself. It's not easy with all the hard muscles in front of me.

Up close, Wes's eyes have flecks of gold dancing in them. He has a small scar cutting his right eyebrow. And his lips. Those cupid's-bow lips look so kissable, I have to fight myself not to lean forward and close the distance between us.

This is bad. This is so bad. I can't be attracted to the person I'm writing about. And that thought throws a bucket of ice water over me. Smoothing my hand down my shirt, I extend my hand.

"Sorry about that. I'm Finn Anderson from the *Berkeley Tribune*."

Wes eyes my hand, like he's uncertain about me, before reaching out his own hand. But even that slight touch has sparks shooting up my arm, causing me to yank my hand back. I need to get back on solid ground. A solid, *professional* ground. "So you're the one that's going to be following my every move?"

Wes crosses his arms. I make the mistake of letting my eyes drop from his arms, farther down to the trail of hair leading to the impressive bulge in his swim trunks. There's not enough time to drink him in before someone is coming up to us.

"I see everyone has met." Damien claps Wes on the shoulder. "Let's get a few more dives in, and then we need to get ready for the event tonight. Sorry, Finn. We're throwing you off into the deep end."

"Wh-what event?" I stutter, not doing well to keep my cool.

"Sorry, I thought Harry must have filled you in. We have a sponsor dinner tonight that we're going to have you attend. Good chance to see everyone outside the pool,"

Damien says, pulling the team away from where I'm standing in the shadows of the boards.

I blow out a breath. "Not a problem. If you send me the details, I'll be sure to be there on time."

Spinning on my heel, I walk back to where I left my bag. I need a minute to breathe fresh, chlorine-free air to reset my equilibrium after that thirty-second meeting with Wes.

I didn't know what to expect when Harry gave me this assignment. I figured days would be spent at the pool. But I guess I don't have the first clue as to what goes into Olympic diving.

These next few weeks are going to test everything I have. Because with Wes? Somehow I think this assignment might be life changing in more than one way.

Chapter Four

WES

"Does he have to come tonight?" I adjust my tie as I finish getting ready in the locker room, with no time to go home before the event tonight.

"We talked about this before, Wes." Damien gives me a long-suffering sigh. "This is important for you. You've all but fallen out of the public's awareness, and you'll need their support ahead of qualifiers."

I crack my neck, running my hand over my well-styled hair. "And yet, I've always made it work before."

"What's the real issue here?" Damien crosses his arms, giving me a hard glare. Having worked with him for the last few years, he knows there's more going on.

"I don't want my entire personal life splashed across the news. I don't need that hanging over my head as I go into qualifiers. Did you think of that?"

"He works for the *Tribune*, not *TMZ*." I fight the eye roll I want to give Damien.

"Doesn't mean he won't use me to get ahead," I grumble under my breath.

"Just keep an open mind, okay?"

An exasperated sigh leaves my lips as I follow Damien out to the car taking us to the team dinner for the evening. Every year, one of the big sponsors of our team hosts a team dinner as a way to flex their influence. Do I like it? It's not my favorite thing, but it's something that comes with the territory.

The ride to the restaurant is quiet, Damien leaving me to my thoughts. It's so much more than the possibility this Finn character could air my personal life. It's the feeling that the world might see that I won't ever get back to where I was before.

What if I go through all of this, and I never get back to where I was? Not once in my life have I ever been worried about my diving performance. But I've never had to come back from an injury. The uncertainty coursing through me is new. Damien has done a good job coming up with a return plan, so I shouldn't be concerned, but I can't help it.

"Ready to go?" Damien claps me on the shoulder, pulling me from my thoughts. The low lights of the restaurant gleam in front of us, the entire place reserved for the team.

The valet opens the door, and standing out on the patio by himself is Finn. I hate that I notice him first thing. I don't want to notice him. He's only here to make my life more difficult.

Focus, Wes. Focus.

"I didn't think you'd come." Simone's loud voice draws Finn's eyes to me. Mine linger for only a second before turning to the woman now linking her arm through mine.

"I can play nice." I decline the proffered glass of wine as we enter the buzzing restaurant. Coaches, teammates, and executives mingle with each other. It's meant to be a casual event, but also a chance to have us win over the bigwigs to renew sponsorships.

"And are you going to play nice with your new shadow?" Simone takes a long pull of the champagne in her glass.

"As long as he plays nice." I grab a glass of water sitting on the bar and take a gulp, the cool liquid sliding down my throat.

"Make sure you do." Simone nods behind me to Finn, who is now approaching us. I don't want to appreciate the view, but I can't help it—the way his suit fits him and the glasses hide his eyes.

"Hi there." Finn's voice is nervous as he approaches us.

"Evening." I take another sip of my water, trying not to focus on the man in front of me. The man who has all the power in this newfound relationship.

"You clean up nice, Finn." Simone's voice is too perky for me.

"You look very nice, as well," Finn replies with all the politeness in his voice. His eyes shift from Simone, roving over me in an obvious perusal. I hide the smile behind my drink, liking it too much.

"Have you ever been to anything like this?" Simone asks, keeping the conversation going.

"This would be my first. Is this normal for you guys?" Finn asks Simone, but his eyes are on me.

"We do them every so often. If it means we get to keep training the way we do, then I'll gladly do it." My eyes don't move from Finn's. It feels like a test. I know my reputation used to precede me. I usually had a different guy on my arm for every event. It never bothered me.

But now, under Finn's watchful eye, it makes me itchy.

"Wes. I have a few people I want you to meet." Damien grabs my elbow, steering me over to a couple of bigwigs.

"Don't worry, I'll take care of him." Simone winks at me as she moves with Finn to the other side of the bar.

"Put on your schmoozing face. We want to make sure these guys donate more to the program," Damien whispers in my ear. It's not anything I don't know. It's important for the program's finances, because otherwise, we wouldn't get to do what we do.

I smile and shake hands. Answer questions about my injury—questions that should be considered intrusive, but I answer anyway.

And all night, my eyes track Finn. It's not like I want to, but his presence has thrown me off. I don't like not knowing what he's going to write about me.

"How you doing, superstar?" A guy, no older than twenty, approaches me when I've finally escaped to the quiet of the bar. I give him a small smile, hoping he takes the hint.

"Want to grab a drink later?" I don't miss the lust in his words. But the man desperately flirting with me doesn't hold my attention.

"Sorry, I have training tomorrow." My voice is even, my hint not taken.

"You sure? I can be fast." He drags a finger up my arm. It does nothing to me.

Now I really wish I had something stronger to drink. Not exactly a ringing endorsement. I shrug, his hand falling back to his side.

"Training doesn't allow for a lot of fun."

"Your loss then."

He walks off with a huff, and I let out a deep breath now that he's gone.

"Do you always attract this much attention?"

Shit. Finn's voice behind me is like a bucket of cold

water being dumped on me. Not because anything happened, but because of how he could spin it.

"Comes with the territory, I guess." I meet Finn's gaze, a curious look hidden behind those black glasses.

"Does it distract you from training?"

I've been paying attention to him all night. Not in the thick of things, but not a wallflower either. He's observant, which sets my teeth on edge.

"I don't let it."

"You're pretty confident in that statement." Finn swallows the last of his own drink.

"I've been sidelined for the last few months. Do you really think I'd let anything stand in my way now?" I pierce Finn with a punishing look. He's known me for all of a few hours. I don't want him getting the wrong impression of me. "The games are about a year away now. Nothing will get in my way."

Finn throws his hands up in defense. "Okay. Good to know."

An edginess buzzes through my skin. I'm used to being in control. But if the last few months have taught me anything, it's that I'm not as in control as I would like to be. Especially now around Finn.

"You haven't watched a full day of practice yet. You'll see."

"I'm excited to see what you have to show me."

"We start early," I warn.

Finn's eyes practically sparkle as he sets his empty glass on the bar behind me. The warm scent of his cologne overwhelms me. I hate that I notice it.

"Then I'll see you bright and early."

Chapter Five

FINN

"**A**re you ready for your first real day?" Melissa's voice is too perky for this early in the morning. I didn't want to give anyone any reason not to like me, so I am getting to the pool at the same time as the team.

After a late night spent at the restaurant with Wes and his team, my head was swirling. It doesn't take an idiot to see that Wes is wary about having me around.

I know my focus should be on Wes and his diving, but when that guy was flirting with him, I couldn't help the feelings that flowed through me. After he was so cagey when turning down the guy at the bar, I went home and fell down the Internet rabbit hole.

Event after event.

Man after man.

It was hard to unsee. The type of man on his arm at these swanky events was not me.

I didn't like it, but it will help me keep Wes on the professional side of things.

"I just hope I don't fall in the pool," I mumble to

myself. I down the rest of my coffee before setting the empty cup in the sink. "Wish me luck."

"Play nice with all the divers." Melissa waves her fingers in my direction as I leave for the diving center.

My head is swimming with everything I've learned in the last twenty-four hours. Harry essentially gave me free rein when he assigned me this story. It would be so easy to write an article on Wes and the parade of men that he's been seen with in the past.

With the way Wes left me last night, I have a feeling it's what he expects.

But I don't want to take the easy way. The easy way won't pave a new road for me. It won't be writing articles that mean something.

Pulling into the facility, I take a deep breath, steeling my nerves.

"No one scared you away?" Damien asks as I walk into the locker room.

"Not yet. I was hoping to grab a word with you before the day gets started, if that's okay."

Damien crosses his arms, leaning against the wall behind me. "Sure thing. What's up?"

"I know Wes isn't too sure about having me here, so I want to know if there's anything that's off-limits before I start."

Damien's brow furrows, assessing me. "Since when do reporters ask for permission?"

A laugh escapes my lips. "I'm still a visitor here. I don't want to step on any toes by going where I'm not allowed."

"You know this was my idea, right? Having you follow Wes's journey back to the Olympics."

I nod. "Harry told me. But I still want to be respectful."

"If Wes gives you any trouble, talk to me, but you've

got an all-access pass as far as I'm concerned. I think you'll be a good influence on him."

"And how's that?" I grasp the strap of my messenger bag, still trying to get a read on Damien.

"As much as Wes's focus needs to be on diving, I'm worried that if he gets tunnel vision again, he might hurt himself and not be able to come back."

"Is that what happened last time?" There wasn't much information on Wes's injury that I could find before I got here. It's still a bit of a mystery.

Damien throws his hands up in defense. "That's his story to tell. But just know that I'm excited to have you here."

With a slap to the shoulder, he's gone.

And I'm left more bewildered than ever.

I know you must be sitting there, reading this article, wondering what I'm doing talking about the Olympics when they aren't until next summer. Most of us don't pay attention to Olympic sports unless it's during the games themselves.

But the NorCal Diving Team, and one diver in particular, will be attempting a comeback to the highest peak of the sport.

Olympic hopeful Wes Cooper has been the diamond of the NorCal Diving Team for the last thirteen years. This past spring, an unfortunate rupture to his Achilles tendon sidelined him during the prime qualifying season.

As Cooper looks forward to the Olympic qualifiers and the games themselves, Berkeley Tribune readers will have an all-access pass into his road to the big event. Don't worry if you don't know anything about diving. I'm learning as I go too.

And if we're lucky, we'll all be experts come next summer. I will be bringing you behind the scenes to training, events, and more as Cooper looks to bring home the gold medal.

Chapter Six

FINN

My nerves are boundless today. After my first article ran yesterday, I'm anxious to see Wes. To see what he thinks. Popping a lemon candy in my mouth, I try to calm down. No one is paying any attention to me, not that they should be. That has to be a good sign, right?

I thought I would be bored with this assignment, watching Wes train. But the dedication he—everyone here, really—shows the sport is palpable.

"How are things going over here with my favorite reporter?" Wes asks, walking over to me. I look around, making sure it's me he's talking to. I set myself up at a table in the corner. An easy enough spot to observe everything but stay out of the way. Scratching my jaw, I make sure I'm not drooling. Wes looks good enough to eat.

"Favorite reporter?" I set my pen down, rolling up my shirtsleeves in the steamy gym, giving him what I hope is a hard stare.

Wes shrugs his shoulders. "You did a good job with your first article."

I quirk my brows up at him. "You read it?"

"Had to see what you were writing. It's hard to know what you're getting with reporters."

I snort. "Hopefully I can change your mind about reporters. We're not all bad."

"I know that, but it's hard for me to trust people."

"And why's that?" I lean forward, resting my elbows on my knees.

Wes leans against the wall, an easy stance. "Because you never know if people are with you for the right reasons. I've been burned in the past, so I'm cautious as to whom I let in my life."

"And you thought I'd be a sleazy reporter."

Wes gives me a bashful look. "What do you say? We can start over and go from here."

I stand, taking a step closer to Wes. "Sounds like a good plan to me."

A smile curls Wes's lips up. I hate how sexy it makes him look. "Good. So what do you want to know?"

"Is this what a typical training day is like?" I wave my hand in the direction of the weight room, trying to distract myself from the god of a man in front of me.

"For the most part, yeah. Weight room, practice boards, then in the pool."

"Practice boards?"

"Yeah, want to come see?" Wes thumbs behind him.

I grab my pen and notebook, trailing behind Wes, doing my best not to stare at his ass. Wes leads me to a large foam pit with diving boards lining the sides.

"This is where you do practice dives?" Blocks of orange and red line the small space.

"We can work on form here instead of doing it in the pool. It's easier, and we can correct any issues faster." Wes shrugs his shoulders.

"Does it hurt?"

"You tell me." Wes bends over, throwing one of the blocks at me, but I'm not fast enough. It smacks me square in the face.

"Warn a man next time," I shout, blocking it too late. "Maybe my next article should be on how you need to be on the defensive while practicing."

A smooth burst of laughter escapes Wes's lips. "Is this how you're going to keep me in line?"

"I doubt anyone can keep you in line."

He lifts a well-muscled shoulder in a shrug. "Damien tries, but it doesn't always work out well for him." Wes strips off his shirt, chucking it at me. The smell of sweat and fresh laundry is strong. "Want to watch up close?"

"Anything to help me with my article." I try to play it cool. Wes struts over to the board. With the grace of a swan, he propels himself off the board, doing a complicated move as he lands with an oomph in the pit.

"How'd that look?" Wes gives me what I'm learning is his trademark grin. Confident, but not cocky.

"If I were a judge, ten out of ten."

"Ouch. I wouldn't make it out of the pool with that score."

I furrow my brows. "Is that not good enough?"

Pushing out of the pit, Wes turns his eyes on me. "If I only got ten points, I'd be cut."

Fixing my glasses, I stare at the ground. "Oh. Well, I'd hate for you to be disqualified."

"Relax." A strong hand grips my shoulder. "I'll make sure you know all the ins and outs of diving by the time I'm done with you."

"How long did it take for you to learn all these different moves?" I wave a pen around in the direction of the pit.

"It came naturally to me I guess. I was always active as

a kid, but it wasn't until a diving event at the school my mom worked at that I started diving. After that, it was a good way to get all my energy out."

"So your parents didn't throw you off a diving board when you were little to see if you were good at it?" A smirk plays on my lips.

"Does anyone really do that?"

"Isn't that how some people try to have their kids learn to swim?"

Wes shakes his head, eyes taking me in. "Not for me, no. I'm actually a pretty crappy swimmer."

"Really?" Shock colors my face.

"Really. I swim a distance of maybe twenty feet from the point I enter the pool to the side. I don't have to be good at that. I'm a diver."

"So not a swimmer."

"See, you're a quick learner. I have no doubt you'll know everything there is to know about diving here soon."

"We'll see about that. Now, what do you do once you're done in here?"

Wes grabs my forearm, dragging me past the training pit to the weight room, ignoring the heat zipping up my arm at the small contact. "Now, I'll hit the weights until I get into the pool later this afternoon."

"And you're able to do all of this with your injury?"

Wes glances down at his foot, to the faint scar that is hardly noticeable on the back of his heel. "I had a lot of physical therapy to get me to where I am today. Damien put together a plan for me so I don't go too hard too fast."

"Is there a risk of reinjuring it?"

I keep my eyes on the pad in front of me as Wes flexes his leg muscle. It's an innocent enough move, but one that won't keep my thoughts in the professional realm. "There's a chance, but not a very high one. I'd more likely injure myself another way instead of tearing it again."

"And you knew you wanted to come back after injury?"

Resting his hands on his hips, Wes turns to give me his full attention. "Why wouldn't I? I still have a lot of diving left in me."

"How long is the average diver's career?"

"It all depends on the person. Some would call it quits after winning the Olympics, others might throw in the towel after an injury."

"And how will you know when to call it a career?"

"Aren't you full of questions today?" Wes aims a smile at me.

"Sorry, too personal?"

He shakes his head, moving to the pull-up bar to start through a new routine. "Just not something I've thought about."

Muscles flex as he lifts his weight above the bar in controlled motions. You would never know he's returning from injury, but there's a heaviness to him, almost like it's weighing him down.

"If you go to the Olympics next year, will you consider that a win, after all you've been through these past few months, even if you don't win a medal?"

Wes does a few more moves before dropping to the ground. "Hand me that towel, will ya?" he asks, motioning behind me. Grabbing the towel, I toss it his way as he wipes the sweat off his body.

"I think anytime you go to the Olympics, it's considered a win. I want to be able to represent my country at the highest level. It'd be even better if I win a medal."

"Have you won gold before?"

Wes shakes his head. "Not at the Olympics. World

Cups and smaller competitions, yes, but not the Olympics."

"If it makes you feel better, I could never do what you do." I sit on one of the weight machines, resting my arms on my knees.

"You don't want to train to go to the Olympics?"

"I run every now and then, but all you're doing here, no way. It'd crush a weakling like me."

"A weakling like you, hmm?" Wes quirks a brow at me, his eyes roving over me. A full-body shiver racks my body as he takes me in. I like being under his watchful gaze.

"I tried playing sports in middle school, but it turns out, if someone was charging me, I'd run the opposite direction to not get hit."

Wes bursts out laughing. "Is it bad I can picture a little Finn running scared with a football in his hands?"

"Go ahead, laugh it up. But I took one too many soccer balls to the head to want to continue playing sports."

"So running it is then." Wes motions for me to get off the weight bench as he starts on his next set of reps. "Nothing else outside of writing?"

"I'm afraid to tell you what else I like doing. It's not very cool." I adjust my glasses, my tongue darting out to wet my lips as my eyes focus on his biceps. Why is this man so distracting to me?

"Okay, now you have to tell me." Wes rests the bar in the stand, and sits up to look at me.

"Bowling."

"Why would I laugh at that? It's been in contention to be an Olympic sport for a few years now. Maybe you could win a gold in it."

I roll my eyes. "Now I feel like you're making fun of me."

Wes rests his hand on his sweaty chest. "I promise you, I'm not. It really has been considered to be an Olympic sport."

"Then if I ever quit my day job, I'll be sure to let you know."

Chapter Seven

WES

"Is there a reason you didn't want to do this at the pool?" Finn is nervous, adjusting his silverware again. I lean back against the booth, an arm thrown across the back.

"Everyone there is too damn nosey for their own good," I tell him. I wanted to get to know him better away from the pool. Away from the prying eyes of the team. "Simone had you in her sights within minutes."

A smile pulls at his cute lips. Finn stuck out like a sore thumb the day he first came to the pool. His dark, curly hair and bespectacled eyes were hard to miss.

"Have you worked with her long?"

The waitress comes over to take our order, dropping off two waters for us.

"Is this you starting an interview?" I grab my glass, taking a long sip.

His eyes widen beneath his glasses. "No!" he shouts a little too loudly. "No. Sorry."

"Is this your first assignment?" Finn seems green. He

doesn't look like a seasoned reporter who has been around the block.

"I'm not some virgin reporter. I do know what I'm doing."

"Interesting choice of words there." There is something about the man sitting across from me that makes me want to rile him up. Finn is so polished with his finely pressed shirt with the sleeves rolled up, exposing corded forearms.

Finn isn't my usual type. But there is something about him that hit me when I shook his hand. He's clean-cut. Like a delayed act of rebellion, I always go for the wrong type. The bad boys that are easy fucks that don't stick around long. It's always worked out that way for me. I'm too busy focusing on diving to worry about anything else in my life.

"Jesus." Finn slaps his hands over the deepening blush crawling its way up his face. "Contrary to how I've been acting, I've been at the *Tribune* for the last year."

"Sports reporting?"

He shakes his head, a lock of hair falling onto his forehead. "Local beat. Following up on community news and things like that."

"So I'm your first…" I let the "assignment" hang off the end. Finn ignores me completely.

"If you're worried about me doing a good job, you shouldn't be. I think my first article proved that I'm not here for the salacious news."

"You don't want to know about my dating past?" I quirk my brows at him as a blush creeps up his cheeks. I like making the man in front of me off-kilter.

"Is it relevant to your training?"

Slicking my tongue over my teeth, I try to think of a way to make it relevant. I don't know why, but I want this man to know I'm single. The last thing I need to be focusing on now is a relationship, but there's something about Finn that has me wanting to spill all my secrets to him.

"Not particularly, no."

"I may not know much about diving, but I at least know that." Finn adjusts his glasses, a righteous air now about him.

"How much do you know about diving? Aside from not knowing the scoring."

"From what I studied last night? About as much as you jumping off a diving board."

"Platform," I correct.

"Sorry, platform." Finn runs a hand through his hair. His eyes fix on mine. "You might have to teach me a thing or two."

There's heat behind his words. It'd be so easy to take the bait, if only to see that blush creep up over his cheeks again.

"What do you want to learn?" The waitress sets our plates down in front of us. Finn nods to the chicken, rice, and veggies on my plate.

"Like that. How strict of a training diet do you have?"

I watch as he picks up his burger, taking a hearty bite. "I'm religious about what I put in my body during the season. Even more so since my injury."

"Has your diet helped with recovery?" Finn asks, ever the journalist.

"I couldn't train. Was laid up for a few weeks after surgery. I didn't want any more setbacks, so I watched everything I put in my body."

Finn's eyes sweep over me, liquid fire washing over me. I shiver, the first time I've felt anything for anyone in God knows how long, and it's for the most inconvenient person.

"I think I can safely say that you treat your body like a temple."

My lips pull up into a smirk, but Finn doesn't take his eyes off me. It tells me that he can feel this between us, whatever this happens to be.

"Not everyone does. It takes dedication to get where I am."

"How long have you been at this?" Finn runs his hand through his hair again, a nervous habit from what I can tell.

"Thirteen years. I started late, so I was already behind the eight ball."

"When do most people start diving?"

"Before they are ten."

"Ten?" Finn's eyes widen in shock. "You mean ten-year-olds throw themselves off those high platforms?"

I smile to myself, noting his usage of the correct term. "Kids have no fear."

Finn nods his head. "My niece has no fear. The things she does I could never do."

I lean back in the booth, swallowing down the bite I took. "So you're not a risk taker then?"

"I like to live in the safety of my bubble. I don't see anything wrong with that."

"I never said there was."

Finn looks away from me, staring down like the plate in front of him will give him all the answers. "Most people give me grief for it."

"Here's a question for you," I say, leaning across the table. "If you could do anything in the world, what would you do? Don't think about it, just blurt it out."

"Go to the top of the Eiffel Tower."

I laugh. "What's stopping you?"

"I hate heights and would need to work myself up to going to the top."

"So you wouldn't be a good diver then?" I ask.

Finn points his fork in my direction. "There's a difference. One doesn't require throwing myself off it. The other, I'm safely ensconced in a metal contraption."

"Fair point. Have you ever been to Paris?"

Finn shakes his head. "I know it seems basic, but it's something I've always wanted to do."

"You know, I've never actually seen the Eiffel Tower up close, and I've been to Paris three times."

"You haven't?" Finn furrows his brows, piercing me with a confused look.

I shake my head. "Life of an athlete. I've been there for the World Cup, and for such a big competition, I didn't want anything stealing my attention."

"Wow. You really are dedicated to your craft." Finn's voice is full of awe, and now it has a blush creeping up my cheeks.

I shrug. "It's not anything anyone else wouldn't be doing."

"Yeah, but I'm not studying them for a story." Pushing his empty plate away, Finn concentrates on me. It's unnerving.

"What?" I shift under the weight of his gaze.

"Nothing. Just wanting to soak up as much as I can while on this assignment."

"You know, you're going to be tracking my every move."

I watch as Finn swallows, his Adam's apple moving in his throat.

"I will be."

"Well then, track away."

Chapter Eight

WES

"**A**re you ready to learn at my feet?"

Finn's eyes widen as he looks around the room. "What are you getting us into?"

"I'm helping you with your article. Can't write what you don't know."

"I guess that's fair." He settles into the seat beside me in the small office. After Finn told me he doesn't know the first thing about diving, I knew I wanted to be the one to teach him. I just never thought I'd be nervous about it. So nervous, in fact, that it threatens to strangle the warm, chlorinated air right out of my lungs.

"Relax. You'll be an expert in no time," I say, dropping a hand on his forearm. Heat rushes from the tips of my fingers, flowing like lava through me at the slightest touch. Finn must feel it too, as goose bumps break out over his skin.

"Right. Let's get started." He pulls his arm out from under my hand, and I hate the loss of him, even though he's right next to me.

"Okay. Why do you practice gymnastics?" Finn has a

pad of notepaper in front of him, gel pen poised in his hand. I like that he's old school. It fits him, or at least what I've learned of him over the last week.

"It mimics the moves of the dives. The way we twist and contort our bodies."

"Isn't it more stress on your body?"

"You've watched videos of me diving, right?"

Finn nods his head.

"By the time I hit the water, I'm going thirty-five miles per hour. If you don't get the right angle, that's a lot more stress on your body than anything else."

Finn visibly flinches. "And you enjoy doing this?"

I can only shrug. "It's all I've ever known. I wouldn't be doing it if I didn't love it."

"Have you ever hit the water at the wrong angle?"

I laugh, scrubbing my hand over my jaw. "So many times. It's how you learn."

"Have you ever hit the platform?"

"Once. But it was enough. Sidelined me for a month."

"Shit. I can't imagine doing that. Just picturing that happening freaks me out."

"It's rare that it actually happens." I lean back in my chair, gazing at the man next to me. Every time I've met him, he's been perfectly poised, ever the professional reporter that he was sent here to be. Dark jeans, light green button-down with the sleeves perfectly rolled up, and dark-framed glasses. I never thought I'd be attracted to someone like him, someone so polished. But something about him pulls my attention from where it should be. From diving and the Olympics.

"Well, once would be enough for me to not get up on the ten-meter." Finn adjusts his glasses, something I'm coming to learn is his nervous tell.

"Not even if I helped you?" I rest my chin on my hand,

giving him my thousand-watt smile. "Might help you get a better grasp on diving if you try it out."

The answering smirk tells me he doesn't fall for it. "I bet that smile gets you far in life, doesn't it?"

"Doesn't hurt." I shrug my shoulders. "You'd be surprised how freeing it feels once you get up on the ten-meter."

"How does it feel?"

"Like you're in your own world. Everyone is quiet when you're diving, so once I'm up there, I'm laser focused on what I have to do."

"And how do you do it? You're that high up—how do you know where you are in the air when you're diving? You don't get dizzy?"

I try to hide my smile, but I can't. God, this guy couldn't get any cuter. "I pick a spot to focus on before I jump. Keep my mind on what I need to do. After that, it's muscle memory on how many spins or tucks I need to do before I hit the water."

"Do you have a favorite dive?"

"Forward three-and-a-half somersault with one twist. It was the first one that ever won me a World Cup, and it's been my favorite ever since."

"Can you show it to me?" Finn leans forward, his eagerness palpable.

Pulling up my training videos on my iPad, I find the video to show him. It's the video from my first gold medal win from a few years ago. It's the one I've been studying to get back to form. The rip into the pool is perfect, barely any splash.

"Wow. And how high of a score did you get on that one? Hopefully not a ten," Finn says, a smirk pulling at his lips. He's shifted closer to me, the heat swirling around us in the small office.

"Ninety-four point five. You take the difficulty and multiple it by the scores of each judge after you throw out the top two and bottom two. That's how you get your score."

"Much better than my ten."

"If a ten is the highest in your book, I'd take it."

Finn's eyes widen, but I don't miss the lust there. It's been a long time since I've been with anyone. I was too down after my injury to focus on it, and even before then, I was too focused on training. Being with Finn could be dangerous. He doesn't seem like the fling type. And I don't know if I'm capable of giving anyone more right now.

My only goal right now should be diving and getting back in shape. It is. All I've ever wanted is to win gold—to know that my hard work and my parents' dedication to me paid off with something tangible.

I shouldn't be concerned with the sexy reporter who looks at me like he wants to know what it's like to kiss me. Who wants me inside of him.

Finn is worth so much more than a fling. And he deserves so much more than I can give him. So I do the smart thing and pull back instead of pushing forward.

I steel my voice, wiping any hint of attraction away.

"Alright, we've got some more learning to do."

Chapter Nine

WES

"Wes. Great to meet you." The older photographer extends his hand, gripping mine in a firm shake.

"Great to meet you too, Andre." I shift, making room for him to see the man standing behind me. "This is Finn. He's with me today."

Andre's dark brown eyebrows rise in question. "Well, welcome. Our team is still getting the final set worked up, so you can start with hair and makeup." He pats me on the back, dismissing me.

"C'mon. Let's go find where we need to go." I bump my shoulder against Finn as his awestruck gaze absorbs everything around him.

"Is this a normal thing for you?" His hands tighten around his bag, almost as if he needs it to stay grounded. We're only a few weeks into this, and he was just seeming to feel settled at the pool.

I shrug my shoulders as I find the area on set where I'm needed. "Yes and no."

An assistant waves me over to her chair, and I comply, settling in for a long day.

"What do you mean?" Finn asks, pushing his glasses up his nose.

"Sponsorships are still a new thing for Olympic athletes, so it's weird putting myself out there like this. But since we don't get paid unless we win, a man's gotta do what a man's gotta do."

"Wait." Finn holds his hands up as people start powdering my face. "You don't get paid?"

"Nope. A lot of sports don't get sponsorships, so if you're in a smaller sport, you might even work a full-time job."

"Do any of your teammates work full-time?" Shock and confusion swirl in Finn's eyes. I could easily get lost there if my attention wasn't being pulled away by the woman attacking me with a brush.

"No. We're lucky that most of us have outside endorsement deals. Like this one for Modern Sport. A few photoshoots here and there, and they're happy. Plus it's an added benefit that I like the work they do around the world for better paying jobs."

"I'm sorry. I just can't get over that you don't get paid."

"Not unless I win," I correct him.

"How much do you get paid if you win?"

"Depends on the medal, but could be up to forty thousand."

"That's it? So let me get this straight," Finn starts, shifting to stand in front of me. "If you don't have a sponsor, you have to pay for all your training yourself and hope that you can be good enough to medal? And only *then* do you get paid?"

The outrage pouring off him hits me in the gut. It's never been something that I've spent too much time thinking about. With a lot of luck, and breaking out at the right time, I was able to make a name for myself in the diving world. Even though I've never won an Olympic medal, people still recognize my name.

"When you put it like that…" I trail off, letting Finn stew with his thoughts. His jaw tics as anger settles over him.

"I just can't imagine working that hard for something, like you do, and not getting paid. That has to be breaking some sort of labor law."

"You know, you're pretty cute when you're all riled up on my behalf." I settle back in the chair as a brush gets dragged through my hair.

Finn's eyes snap to mine. Any anger he had shrivels up with the heated look he gives me. It sends a shudder down my spine, settling in my groin. It would be a very inconvenient time to get a hard-on with this many people around, ready for me to go shoot in a tiny bathing suit. The pink tinge in Finn's cheeks has me wondering if anything else blushed.

"Well, you have it pretty easy from what I can tell." Finn waves a hand in front of me as I glance in the mirror. The stylist is gelling my hair into place. "It's the people that have to work full-time while training that I'm outraged for. I couldn't imagine working from nine to five and then having to go train."

I prop an elbow on the flimsy armrest, resting my chin on my fist. "Would you want to try training with me?"

"W-with you?" Finn's voice breaks as the stylist leaves the two of us alone.

"Well, I'm not going to pass you off to someone else. Maybe it could give you a unique perspective. See what a day in the life of an Olympian is *really* like."

Finn's mouth opens and closes as nothing comes out.

"For someone who uses his words to make a living, you're sure struggling to find some."

"Do you really think someone like me could keep up with someone like you?"

My eyes trail over Finn, from the denim jeans hugging his legs to the white T-shirt clinging to his chest. It causes an uncomfortable stirring in my gut, one that I'm not quite familiar with but wouldn't mind feeling again.

"Someone like you, huh?"

A small smile tugs at the corner of Finn's lips. "I don't know if you know this, but I'm not exactly the most physical of creatures."

He makes it so easy sometimes. "Not physical, huh? You mean just training, right?"

Finn slaps a hand across his face, rubbing at the corner of his eyes. "Jesus. Why do you get me so worked up?"

"If you really want to get worked up, I can do that." Heat laces my words. There is nothing more that I want right now than to blow this photoshoot off and do exactly that with Finn. To see what he tastes like. Does he taste like those lemon candies he's always sucking on?

"Wes. We're ready for you." The moment is interrupted when the wardrobe woman greets me.

Finn's cheeks are even pinker now as I stand, closing the small space between us. His eyes flit between my eyes and my lips. God, it would be so easy to take him in a kiss in this moment. But I don't want our first kiss to be in the middle of a photoshoot with dozens of people running around.

Because make no mistake, there will be a first kiss with him, if his reaction is anything to go by. I lean closer to Finn, inhaling his scent and fighting every urge I have. "To be continued."

Finn

AS IF WES invading my thoughts earlier wasn't bad enough, I now have to stare at him while his abs are getting oiled down before he starts the shoot.

Eight glorious muscles, all stacked on top of each other in perfect lines. And every time he looks at me, it turns my thoughts from the professional kind I should be having to a dangerous kind.

Those dangerous thoughts have been plaguing my dreams. Every night I imagine what it would be like to trace my tongue over those abs. To take his lips in a kiss that would sear into my brain for the rest of time.

"Alright everyone, let's get this show on the road!" Andre calls from his spot behind the camera. Lights are turned to face Wes, illuminating him like he's the only person in the room.

Camera clicking away, Wes moves his body with all the grace and power he possesses in the pool. The photographer is eating it up, words of praise pouring out of him.

Each turn, each move, has me more fascinated with everything about this life of an elite athlete that Wes leads.

Wes dedicates himself to his training twenty-four/seven. There's no off day. No alcohol. Nothing in his body that could set him back a day. The single-minded focus is something I don't think I could ever possess.

I love what I do. Even on the community beat, I still loved writing. But I have never had focus like Wes. For thirteen years, he's done this. I've been with him all of a few weeks and I'm exhausted.

"Give me a sultry look. Yes. Just like that."

The shift in his face is subtle, but Wes's eyes find mine. The air crackles with electricity as we stare at one another.

His lips part, as if readying himself for a kiss. My tongue darts out on its own, wetting my own lips, as if it'll summon Wes to me and finally, finally, let me taste him.

Just the thought has me wanting to push everyone out of the way and claim what's mine. My dick, choosing the most inappropriate time, pushes against the zipper of my jeans. I try to shift, covering myself, but it's no use. The star of my dreams is putting on the show of his life as the photographer finally calls for a break in shooting.

"Thank God," rushes out of my lips. No one is around to hear me, as I shuffle out of the way and back to the waiting room. Popping a candy in my mouth, I shake my arms, trying to expel some of this nervous energy.

"Great job!" Shouts come through the door as Wes appears. His muscles flex and ripple as his fingers tap against his leg.

The moment Wes steps into the small lounge area, it's just the two of us. My fingers ache to touch him, to see what he feels like. To brush the soft locks of his brown hair off his forehead as I stare into his deep, brown eyes.

"That was quite a performance." The words don't sound like they're coming from me, my voice so full of need, it drops a full octave lower.

"I had some inspiration to help." Wes leans against the wall, propping a foot against it, as he crosses his arms.

"Oh yeah?" My stomach drops as I take a step closer to him. Everything about Wes's posture should say he's blocking me out, but I know better. Studying him these last few weeks, I've learned that every move he makes is intentional. The heat in his eyes tells me he wants me to make the first move.

"Shoots like this can take hours, but he got what he wanted. A few more outfit changes and we'll be good to go." Before I know it, the tips of my shoes are brushing against Wes's bare toes.

"How do you come down from these highs? I wasn't even the one putting on the show, and I feel like I've run a marathon."

"Usually I'll hit the gym after. Always makes me feel better."

"Usually?" I lean closer, resting a hand on Wes's forearm. The heat coming off him is palpable.

"I can think of something I would much rather do today."

Pushing off the door, Wes rests a hand on my shoulder, sending shockwaves through my body. Every thought I've had about why this is a bad idea, on why I shouldn't get involved with someone like Wes, goes out the window as he closes the space between us.

"And what's that?" I can see the faint freckles on Wes's nose and the tiny fractions of light that bounce around in his eyes as he looks at me. The air stills around us as I close the distance.

"Wes. Wardrobe is ready for you."

A beckoning voice has me jumping back from Wes. There's a fury in his eyes as he tries to find the person behind the voice. I rub a hand over my lips, trying to quell the burning need that threatens to explode out of me.

I should be thanking the person who stopped us from kissing. Kissing Wes would be messy. How can I objectively report on him when all I can think about is being with him?

I've spent too many days being around Wes. Maybe a day in the office is just the ticket to snuff out the fire coursing through me. Maybe. Hopefully.

At least, I can try.

Chapter Ten

FINN

"Finn. Give me an update." I trot off behind Harry, heading into his office. "How are things going with Cooper?"

Adjusting my glasses, I hold the notebook to my chest like a shield of armor. "So far, so good." He doesn't need to know that I have dreams about Wes coming out of the pool. The way the water sluices down his body turns me on more than any man ever before him.

"That's it? Not giving me anything else?" Harry pulls off his glasses, sticking one end in his mouth, giving me a thoughtful once-over. "I need more than that."

"My brain is swimming with information. I'm just trying to filter everything out so I give the people what they really want to know." Not the information that I'm dying to know, like if Wes is looking for a relationship. Although with his schedule, I doubt it.

"And has Wes been good?"

I nod. "Yes. Picture of professionalism. Not sure why everyone thought he would be so difficult to work with."

Harry smirks back at me. "Damien tends to be hard on

his athletes to get the best out of them. So glad to hear Wes is being a good sport about it. Have your latest article to me tonight."

"Sure thing." I don't waste another minute and bolt out of Harry's office. Collapsing into the safety of my desk chair, I pull up all the notes and pictures I've been capturing these past few weeks.

It's a reprieve to be in the office today and not surrounded by Wes's intoxicating pull. This is a place where I know I belong, where I feel settled. Sometimes I'll get wrapped up in a story and lose track of time. The training center is a whole different world.

It's not like it hasn't been beneficial, being there with everyone. But being around Wes is exhilarating. I've only known him for a few weeks, and I've learned he is a hard man to ignore. Every time I'm around him, I want to stay around him. He has a way of setting everyone at ease.

I thought he would be a cocky asshole when I met him. Wes oozes confidence so people, including me, can't help but want to be near him. And that makes it difficult, because the opportunity I have here is huge. I have the chance to make a name for myself with this assignment. I shouldn't be falling for the guy I'm writing about. No matter how good he looks in his Speedo.

And it would've been bad if I'd crossed that line at the photoshoot. Because all I wanted to do was capture his lips with mine and see if it would be worth all the fuss and turmoil I'm putting myself through.

What I need is more days in the office to clear my head and remind me why I'm doing this. Because if I have to be around him like I was yesterday, I don't know how I'll be able to stop myself from making a move. Or letting him make one on me.

This will be good. I can clear my head and keep Wes at a distance. Get back to being professional Finn Anderson.

"Anderson!" Harry barks out from his office. "You're going to Vancouver with the team tomorrow. You'll be there for a few days, so head out early and get packing."

Crap. So much for distance.

The Dark Side of Olympic Training
By Finn Anderson

Every four years, the world's focus shifts from whatever we're doing to the Olympics. We come together as one to cheer on our fellow citizens that are representing our country.

But there's a side of Olympic training that not many of us know about. Many of the athletes that we cheer on work full-time jobs outside of training, because without sponsorships, they don't make any money from their sport.

Sure, some of the bigger sports, like swimming and diving, have sponsorships, but that's only if you're the cream of the crop. The crème de la crème.

For the athletes that don't make money on their sport, they have to find the time to train during a full-time job—in addition to paying for their own training.

The Olympics aren't lucrative. US athletes only get paid if they win a medal. And fewer than three percent of Olympians at the games will win a medal. Not great odds.

But the people who love their sport are not doing it for the money. They do it because they love it. Because they wake up and can't imagine not playing every day.

We love being able to cheer on our table tennis and canoe teams every four years, but maybe we can all do more to support them during non-Olympic years. By bringing more attention and awareness to the smaller sports, maybe we can make it easier for our Olympians to do the sports they love.

Chapter Eleven

WES

"Are you excited to be traveling with the team?" I ask, as Finn settles into the middle seat next to me.

"Aside from the whole heights thing, I'm excited."

Something squeezes in my gut. I like knowing that this isn't something Finn has done before. That I get to be the one he experiences this first with. "Have you been to Vancouver?"

He shakes his head. "I've been to Mexico. But that's about it."

"Spring break?" My lips quirk up as he pushes his bag underneath the seat in front of him.

"Is that the only reason you think someone would go to Mexico?" He turns, piercing me with his blue gaze. The way his glasses frame his face has my thoughts turning dirty. Finn's eyes are so expressive. I want to see what they'd look like as I'm pounding into him.

"Is it bad that I'm picturing you drinking cocktails on the beach? Fighting off the advances of other coeds." I'd love to see Finn let loose. To shed this professional demeanor of his, even though it makes me inordinately jealous. I have no claim to this man, but I want him.

Finn lets out a deep belly laugh, one that hits me square in the chest. "I was there for my sister's wedding. They wanted to get married before they had their baby, so they 'eloped.'"

"Is this the sister you live with?" The flight attendant starts going through the safety speech. I've heard it so many times on my travels I could recite it in my sleep.

"It is. She gets free babysitting whenever she needs it, and I have a place to stay until I can save enough to buy a house. Wherever that may be."

My brows furrow in confusion. "You don't see yourself settling down here in Berkeley?"

Finn shrugs his shoulders. "I don't know. I'll go wherever the stories take me. I'm not picky. I want to write something that matters."

"Why does my story matter?" I prop my elbow on the armrest, my gaze moving closer to Finn's.

He fidgets, adjusting his glasses. I like that I make him nervous. Maybe I get under his skin as much as he does mine.

"I haven't decided yet." His eyes grow wide. "Not that you don't matter, but I just haven't figured out why your story will make a difference to the world."

"You really think it will?" The playfulness leaves my voice. It's like Finn landed on everything that has been plaguing me these last few weeks. Last few months actually.

Even before my injury, I knew I was pushing too hard. My sole goal was to win an Olympic gold. I had tunnel vision. Nothing was going to stand in my way—except me. I drove myself too hard and ended up hurting my chances even more. The pressure that I might have screwed up my chances weighs heavily on me.

Finn's warm hand on my forearm brings me back to present. His eyes are right there, lips inches from my own.

"Yes. Whether you like it or not, you're a role model for a lot of people."

I give him a playful push back, jerking back in my seat as the plane takes off speeding down the runway, slowly rising into the air. "I don't know if anyone would call me a role model. I screwed myself in the worst possible way." It's hard to stay positive some days about my situation and how it feels like I'm starting from zero.

"Don't discount me. I know I've only been around you for a few weeks, but I'm not an idiot."

I shift my head to focus on him once again. Something about the way he says it makes me think someone has said it to him before. "I never said you were. I just know that I was the one to put myself in this situation."

"And from what I can tell, you're doing a pretty good job of getting yourself out of it. I couldn't do what you do."

As the plane pulls up from the ground, Finn's hands clench the armrests. "I'm guessing it's the heights thing?"

"I don't know why anyone would want to voluntarily throw themselves off a ten-meter platform, let alone jump out of a plane."

"I don't know. I think you'd make a good diver."

Finn blows out a puff of air. "Now I know you're lying. I'd probably kill myself jumping from that height."

"No one has died in decades."

"You mean someone has died?!" Finn's eyes are as wide as I've ever seen them.

"It was a freak accident in the eighties. I've sustained the occasional concussion while diving, but it's why we practice," I say firmly. I don't know why, but I want Finn to know that this is a safe sport. That I'm safe when I hurl myself off a concrete block thirty feet in the air.

"Then I guess I'll just spend my time as a spectator." He shivers, like he can't imagine doing what I do.

"I'll get you on the boards if it's the last thing I do."

Finn is smiling now, his knuckles no longer clutching the seat in a death grip. "Oh yeah? After one session, will I look like you? Like the Greek god of diving?"

"Greek god, huh?" Finn's face heats. I like making him feel unsteady. "It took years to get this fit. Training for days on end. Strict diets. No alcohol. Not much of a life, really."

"Is that more self-induced? Or is that life common for an athlete such as yourself?" Finn turns on his reporter voice. I know anything we say is fair game. It doesn't irk me as much as I thought. I thought it would be nothing but salacious gossip. But I should know better with Finn. Carrying himself with a grace I wish I possessed outside of the water, he laid down the facts of what he'll be doing these next few months.

"More common than you'd probably realize. Some might never get the opportunity to compete for a medal, but for me, it's the one thing I want in life."

"Not a partner or a family?"

His words hit a hard spot inside me. One that I try not to dwell on too much. "I'm only twenty-seven. There's still plenty of time for that. Plus I might not find someone who wants to put up with this lifestyle."

"I take it you've lost people because of it?" Finn is more perceptive than most.

I nod my head. "A few actually. They didn't like that I wasn't putting them first during the season. This has been my whole life for as long as I can remember. It's so close I can almost taste it."

My words feel like I'm warning Finn. Someone like

Finn is too good to tangle himself with the likes of me. No matter how much I want to wrap myself around him.

"I have faith in you." Finn's voice is strong, clear. It almost wipes out every fear I've been having lately. Like never actually achieving gold.

The words *thank you* get stuck in my throat. The fact that my biggest cheerleader has only known me for a few weeks, yet sees me better than anyone else in my life, should worry me. But it doesn't.

It excites me and lights a fire in my veins that has long been dormant.

It's just a matter of time before it combusts.

Chapter Twelve

FINN

It's been a standard day of training for Wes and the NorCal diving team. The facility in Vancouver is state of the art. It's newer than the one at home in Berkeley. The foam pits are larger with more boards for more divers to practice together.

It's riveting to watch the way they contort their bodies with practiced ease before landing on the squishy blocks below. Every time I watch them feels like the first time. I'm just as excited and nervous when they dive. In the few short weeks I've been with the team, I've seen the dedication they have.

Not just anyone can be in the club. It takes a certain kind of person to join. I'm constantly in awe of this group of people. To have no fear and push yourself like this inspires me in my own career.

I have no idea where I'll end up. I'm a lowly journalist just starting out, trying to make a name for himself. But the more I'm around these people, the more I know I'm not cut out for the local beat. Everyone has to start somewhere, but it strengthens my desire to write something important. Something that matters.

"So is this a lot of what you do?" Dan asks, stretching his arms over his head after hitting the weight benches.

"What do you mean?" My phone and notepad are sitting on the bench next to me.

"I thought you'd be in everyone's faces. Asking questions, snapping photos…that kind of thing."

I snort laugh. "Not in the slightest. Wes is my main focus. It's easy to sit back and observe him."

Dan looks between the two of us. Wes is at the bar, doing pull-ups. Sweat is dripping down his body. I still remember the first time I jacked off to that image. I couldn't help myself. The man is delectable.

"He makes your job hard, doesn't he?" The sarcasm is evident in his voice. It's nice getting to know Wes's teammates during this assignment too.

"I've had worse assignments." I grab my phone, trying to distract myself and not show my true feelings for Wes. Dan doesn't need to know them.

"Mmhmm. I bet." Dan grabs the water bottle on the bench and starts to back away. "If you ever need a good story or two about him, you know where to find me."

"Everything okay over here?"

Wes startles me, my phone dropping to the floor. "Just peachy."

I close my eyes, wishing I could draw those words back in.

"Peachy, eh?" Wes drags a towel down his chest. His abs contract with every breath he takes. It takes everything I have not to reach out and drag a finger over each one. To commit them to memory so I have something to use in my spank bank.

"Just observing you in your natural habitat."

"And? Is it any different than home?" Wes questions.

I purse my lips, shaking my head from side to side. "Yes and no. I don't know if I've learned more about what you do over these last few weeks, but your movements are more graceful to me."

"There's definitely an art to it."

"Do you have a favorite position?"

"Just one?"

I mentally smack myself in the forehead. I know I've already asked him this, so I don't know what it is about this man that has me saying these things around him. I'm by no means the coolest person in the room, but around Wes, I'm a blubbering idiot.

"You know what I mean." My cheeks are hot, and not from the temperature in the room. Embarrassment floods through me.

"I do. But I'd like to go over your favorite positions."

Instead of being able to put distance between the two of us, I have been thrown right into the lion's den. I had one day of reprieve from Wes before being with him twenty-four/seven for the next few days of training camp.

And today has been anything but easy. Wes has been working in the pool, and seeing him pull himself out, the water sluicing down every nook and cranny? I hate to say I'm jealous of the water.

"Maybe you should go continue working on your form. I'd hate to be a distraction for you."

Wes flashes me a blinding smile. I hate what it does to my insides. "You're anything but a distraction, Finn." He winks as he walks back, spinning on his heel to return to the pool deck.

I blow out a breath, sinking farther back into my seat.

This is getting dangerous. I'm a professional writer. I should be able to control myself. I shouldn't be taken with the first handsome man that I work with. But it's more than just his face.

He shows more dedication to his craft than most people I know. It's the way his teammates look to him for leadership. I've only been around a few weeks, but I already know I'm going to be cheering for him long after I'm gone.

I watch as he goes back to the pool, working off one of the lower boards. I'm not the only one that stops to pay attention as he twists and contorts his body as he dives. He's messing around with some of the other divers, doing easy moves. At least, easy from what I can tell.

After each dive, Damien is right there, critiquing what he's doing. And Wes takes it with a smile. Every so often, his eyes find mine.

I can't take my eyes off him.

I wouldn't want to even if I could.

Damn Wes and the powerful spell he's cast on me.

Because all I want is him.

Chapter Thirteen

WES

"You're cheating!" Simone bellows out.

"It's not my fault you're terrible at cards," Dan says, a smirk playing on his mouth. I love nights like this while away at training camp. So often we go our separate ways, but I love bonding with my teammates and letting them get to know Finn better.

I like having him around. And the more he's around, the more I like the idea of him being around.

"There's no way you're good enough to win three straight rounds." She sips on her seltzer, throwing her cards down in frustration.

"Is this what you guys always do when you're away?" Finn whispers in my ear. His hand swirls the whiskey he's drinking in the glass. He's barely touched it as we've been playing poker all night with the team.

"Sometimes yes, sometimes no. Depends on where we are. If the Canadian team were here, we'd go out to dinner with them, but they're training in Toronto."

"You're friends with them?" Finn looks floored that we're friends with another team.

"Of course we are. Diving is an individual sport, so if you screw up, it's on you."

"And since you're not doing synchro, there's no one to yell at." Finn nods his head in understanding.

"Even then, you make friends with everyone because there's a lot of downtime between events. We train with them all over the world, so it's fun seeing people you don't usually get to see."

Finn looks around the small hotel room we're holed up in. "I keep learning something new about diving every day I'm around you."

"I like that you're learning something new." I shift in my chair, my arm settling next to Finn's. The heat coming through his shirt has my blood stirring. A hot craving boils inside me for this man.

It's more than lust. It's more than need. I crave him, all of him, with a bone-deep desire, all from the merest of touches.

And based on the way Finn's eyes are focused on the spot of contact, I know he feels it too.

The small room starts to get even smaller. I'm no longer invested in the mindless game we're playing to unwind.

"I think I'm calling it a night." I give a not-so-subtle knock into Finn's shoulder, signaling he should leave too.

"Oh, uh, yeah. Me too," he stutters. If I didn't want him so badly, I'd laugh.

I stand, adjusting my pants to hide the half-chub I'm now sporting. My teammates are too engrossed in the round they're playing to pay any attention to us or to notice us leaving.

Shoving my hands in my pockets, I have to hold myself back from attacking Finn the moment we leave the room.

I'm good as we make our way to the elevator, even as Finn's eyes keep drifting to me.

But when the elevator comes and we're in the small space?

Finn's cologne makes it hard to breathe, and I cave.

"It was nice getting to know everyone better tonight," he says. His fists are balled up at his sides, and it snaps my composure.

Punching the stop button of the elevator, I turn to Finn and see his brows draw together in confusion. I back him up against the elevator wall, my hands landing on either side of his head.

"What are you doing?" Finn's voice is breathy as it heaves out of his chest.

"Do you know how crazy you make me?"

The vein in Finn's neck throbs. The way it pulses makes me want to strike like a snake. He opens his mouth a little, his eyes drifting down to mine. His tongue darts out to wet his lips, and I'm a goner.

Wrapping my hands around his neck, I claim his lips with mine. They're soft, just like I knew they would be. The stubble scratches against my palms as I tilt his head, a small gasp escaping from Finn, allowing me to plunder his mouth.

My dick is hard in my pants, so hard I'm afraid I might come from the friction of my boxers. Finn's hands wrap around my wrists as I continue my exploration of his mouth. His tongue pushes back against mine, fighting for power.

The taste of whiskey will forever be burned on my tongue. I drop one hand away from Finn's neck, running down the material of his shirt. Just like I expected, when I reach his jeans, I cup his hard cock, threatening to break free of its denim prison.

"Totally worth the fuss," Finn murmurs.

Breaking the kiss, I pull back, meeting his gaze. "What?"

Finn's eyes are filled with liquid lust, flowing between us as I rub his hard-on. "Don't worry about it."

My voice is raspy. I don't look away from him. There are a million reasons why I shouldn't be doing this. But every single one flees my mind. "I want you, Finn."

"Can it not be in the elevator?" His hand squeezes my wrist, still locked in his hold. Not letting him let me go, I drop my hand from the bulge in his pants, then reach back and pop the red button back into place. The elevator jolts into action. Finn and I stay still, our eyes locked.

The temperature in the small space is hot. A single spark could ignite the air around us. When the elevator dings, Finn steps forward. He's vibrating with need. Releasing my hold on him, I lead us back toward my room. The hallway feels endless. All I want is to feel Finn's skin on mine. To know what it feels like to be balls deep inside of him. To see his face as he comes.

I bump into the door, not realizing how close we are. Pulling out the key, my breath hitches as Finn crowds my space. I stick the key in the slot, but I'm met with a red light. Trying again, I get the same results. A frustrated growl leaves my mouth as Finn's warm lips find my neck.

"Need some help?" His hands wrap around me, one drifting down to my own hardened cock. I throw my head back against his shoulder.

"If you keep touching me like that, we won't make it into the room." But my words fall on deaf ears. Finn's hands drift under the cotton of my T-shirt.

"Do you know how much I've fantasized about these abs of yours?" His words are whispered in my ear, his lips tracing the shell. "I've wanted to run my tongue along each one since the day we met."

"Fuck." I jam the key into the slot and am met with a green light. Forcing the door open, I pull Finn in and shove him against the door. "God, you're sexy."

I don't know who moves first when our lips meet, but the tension explodes. I sink into the kiss and the way Finn is holding me as he takes command. I've never been so taken with someone before that I could get lost in a kiss for hours.

Sweet and sexy Finn. The way he is turning me on with just his tongue has me grinding against him, my hard cock rubbing against his.

His strong hands find my hair, tugging me back. The fiery look in his eyes tells me this is going to be a night I remember. "Take off your shirt." The rasp in his voice is heady as I yank my shirt over my head.

I love that shy, quiet Finn is now totally in command of me. Not for long, but I love the way he wants to dominate me.

His eyes rake over me, the sensation settling low in my groin. He's only touched my lips, but I know that when Finn finally touches me, bare skin to bare skin, it will be life changing.

"It's not fair you look this good naked." Finn drags a finger down my stomach before sweeping it over each ab. "How I'm the lucky guy that gets to see you like this…" he trails off as he slowly sinks to his knees.

Finn's mouth trails a path on his way down, flicking each tight nipple. I hiss, the sensation making it hard to keep from coming. I think of my diving moves, because I'm not coming until I'm buried inside Finn's pert ass.

"I could write an entire article on these abs." Finn moves his hands to my hips, as his lips brush against the taut skin of my stomach. Each warm pass of his lips is driving me closer to the brink.

"I don't know if anyone would be interested in that," I breathe out. My voice sounds different to my own ears, like I'm light years away, wrapped up in Finn's orbit.

"Oh, I believe they would." Finn looks up at me as his tongue swipes across one. "With how sculpted they are." His teeth bite into one. My hips thrust, as my dick needs more attention. Finn notices but doesn't seem to care. His sole focus is on my stomach. "How they ripple and flex every time you get out of the water. God, Wes, you're a wet dream, and you don't even know it."

I can't wait any longer. I pull Finn up my body and back him farther into the room. "It's time we make that dream become a reality, don't you think?"

Finn

THE HUNGRY LOOK in Wes's eyes should alarm me. But it makes me hard, harder than I can ever remember being. Throwing me down on the bed, Wes stands over me, and I take another moment to appreciate the specimen of a man in front of me. He's even better up close. The feel of his abs under my lips is something I'll never forget. Wes pulls a condom and lube from his wallet and drops it on the bed beside me. But when he drops his jeans and boxers, his dick springing free, everything is wiped from my brain.

"Cat got your tongue?" Wes gives himself a lazy stroke as he stalks toward me. I'm his prey. I shudder at the thought of being at his mercy. I want Wes to take me in every way possible. To feel him fill me up and explode inside of me.

"Just thinking of all the ways we can do this tonight." I lick my lips, my mouth suddenly dry as Wes fits himself between my legs.

"Oh yeah? And would one of them have my cock in your mouth?"

Arrogance like his would usually be a turnoff. But something about the way Wes carries himself has me reaching out, covering his hand with mine.

"Are you on PReP?" I ask, not taking my eyes off him.

He nods. "I am, and have been tested recently. You?"

"Yes."

It's all the information I need. I lean closer, rubbing the head of his dick against my lips. The saltiness on the tip has my tongue seeking the source. Licking the slit, I pull Wes's dick into my mouth. I hum around it, opening my mouth wide to accommodate his size.

"This is even better than I imagined." Wes cups my jaw as I suck him farther back into my mouth. His cock pulsates against my tongue as I pull back. My hand slicks up and down, spreading the wetness down. The tip is an angry red as I kiss up and down his shaft.

Groans and moans from Wes make it hard to stop. As much as I want to feel him inside me, I love this power I have over him. The god of a man I'm used to seeing on a daily basis is now at my mercy. Sucking in a deep breath, I take Wes into my mouth as far as I can. I nearly gag, but don't stop, pumping up and down his thick length.

"I can't take it anymore." Wes thrusts his hands into my hair, pulling me off him. "I need to be inside you."

Wes's dick glistens with my spit. I reach down, rubbing my own aching dick.

"Get naked." The command is back in Wes's tone.

There's nothing that would stop me from stripping down and offering myself up to him without hesitation. Grabbing the back of my shirt, I pull it over my head. I throw the offending material at Wes as I stand, stepping into his space.

"Please, don't stop." Wes takes a step back, inhaling my scent from my shirt.

Opening my belt, I unbutton my jeans and slowly snick the zipper down. Wes's eyes don't leave my hands, lest he miss a second of what I'm doing. I push my jeans down, toeing off my shoes before kicking them to the side. I reach for my boxer briefs, but Wes stops me.

"Don't you dare. That's for me."

"Didn't you want me to get naked?" I leave my hands under the waistband as Wes walks toward me.

"I changed my mind." A strong hand on my shoulder pushes me back on the bed. The heat swirling around the two of us is almost too much to bear. "I want to peel these off you with my teeth."

Wes leans over me, forcing me back onto the bed. His clean scent, with the barest hint of chlorine, is heady. It's one hundred percent Wes. His lips suck on the tender skin of my neck as he slinks down my body with practiced ease. The control I thought I had is being sucked out by Wes as he moves lower, sinking his teeth into every nook and cranny on my body.

"Please, Wes. I'm dying."

"Now, now, Finn. Just you wait." He smirks up at me as he tongues the edge of my briefs. I'm aching, my cock dripping with need. My fists ball into the soft duvet, not getting the friction where I need it most.

Hands trace a path down my sides as Wes sits back on his feet. "You're beautiful, Finn. The sexiest man I've ever been with."

Wes's words settle over me, distracting me from the hand moving up my thigh. The warmth of his words settles in my chest. Every day, I see brute strength come out of Wes as he throws himself into his training. However, the man I'm seeing now has more tender edges. It's like he's showing a side to me that no one else is privileged to.

"Are you still with me?" Wes pulls me back to where we are. To the hotel room in Vancouver with him on his knees.

"Yeah." I nod my head, my voice quiet.

"Good." Wes hooks a finger in my briefs. "Because I'm about to blow your mind."

Wes's teeth nip at my hip as he finally—*finally*—frees my dick from its cotton prison. He traces a calloused fingertip along the throbbing vein.

I thrust up, needing more from him. "Please, Wes. I don't know how much more I can take."

"Don't worry. I'll take care of you." He places a kiss on the tip of my dick, grabbing the lube next to him and coating his fingers. I pulse in his hands in anticipation of feeling him where I want him.

Wes pays special attention to my dick as a warm, slick finger presses against my tight ring. Relaxing against him, I welcome the intrusion. The slight sting gives way to pleasure as Wes pushes in deep.

A garbled mess of words rushes out of me.

"Doing okay?" His warm breath is at my hip as his hand continues working its way up and down my engorged shaft.

"Yes. God, yes."

"Good." Wes pulls out slightly, taking me in his mouth at the same time he thrusts his finger back inside me, hitting that deep spot that feels so good.

"Wes. Oh God, don't stop." I feel a second finger as

Wes works me open, driving me higher and higher, stretching me in the best way. The initial burn is gone. All I feel is pleasure firing through my veins.

"Are you ready?" Wes's thumb brushes over the tight skin under my balls. The contact is explosive.

"Ready."

Wes's eyes find mine as he shifts between my legs. The sound of a condom packet tearing echoes throughout the small room. Fervent need burns bright in Wes's brown eyes.

"Scoot up." Wes taps the outside of my leg as I center myself on the bed. Putting more lube on his hand, Wes coats himself before crawling over me.

"I can't believe you're finally mine." Wes cups my face, kissing me fiercely. The need behind this kiss is more than I can handle right now.

"Then make me yours." Wes lines his slicked cock up and gently eases in.

Wes swallows my gasp as he slowly pushes in to the hilt. Wrapping an arm around his shoulder, I hold him to me, adjusting to his size. A burning need stirs low in my gut as I hook a leg around Wes, urging him to move. Dropping his forehead to mine, he sets a punishing pace.

I clench around him at every thrust, welcoming him as he pegs my prostate. My arousal leaks all over my stomach as he takes my cock in his hand.

"I can't wait to see you explode."

The tight grip he has on me has my balls drawing up tight, ready to unleash.

"I'm almost there." I lean up, searching for his lips with mine. The sweet taste of his lips is a contrast to the fiery need burning between us. His tongue matches his thrust, pushing me over the cliff. I yank my lips from his, shouting my release. Cum coats my chest as Wes pummels into me.

"Yes. God, you are so damn sexy." Wes's hair falls in his face as his corded neck flexes, his own orgasm just out of reach. My nails dig into his shoulders, pulling him closer as I ride out this high like I've never experienced before.

"Let me feel you come." I suck on Wes's neck as he grabs hold of my leg, giving himself better access.

"Fuuuuck," Wes growls, collapsing on top of me as he pulses inside me, filling the condom. Sweat and cum mix together on my chest as Wes stills on top of me, our heavy breathing now the only sound in the room.

"Give me a minute," he whispers after our heart rates have gone back to normal. Wes kisses my neck, gently easing out of me before going to the bathroom and taking care of the condom. He comes back a minute later, wash cloth in hand to clean me up. Chucking it behind him when he's done, he pulls the duvet back for us, wrapping me in his arms.

"Finn. I don't know what to tell you, but that was...wow."

A smile burns my face as I nestle into the crook of his arm, a place that is now my favorite to be.

"Wow indeed."

Chapter Fourteen

WES

"What's all this?" Coming out of the bathroom, I notice a tray of food now fills the table by the window.

"I figured since you have a late start today, we could have breakfast here in the room." Finn pushes his glasses up his nose, his naked torso still on display for me. The view has me hardening in my boxers as I remember what it felt like to have him under me.

"Is this the only option for breakfast?" I step behind him, wrapping my arms around his hips. The tips of my fingers flirt with the band of his boxer briefs. His skin is still warm, heating my own body.

"I'd say there could be more, but I also know how much sustenance you need for training before we leave today."

"You're no fun." I drop a kiss to his neck, inhaling his scent.

Smacking my hand, he steps out of my arms and makes a plate for himself. "Someone has to be responsible. I don't want to be the cause of you losing out on a medal."

"Trust me, I'm the only one who will be in my way."

"What do you mean?" Finn pops a grape into his mouth, sitting on the chair.

"The whole reason I'm injured was because of my own dumb mistakes."

"What happened?"

FIVE MONTHS *Earlier*

"ALRIGHT, *Wes. That's good. Let's call it a day."*

I shake my head, turning to face Damien at the end of the tumble mat. "Something feels off. The twist in the middle doesn't feel right."

"Let's leave it for tomorrow. You've put in a long day"

"Just a few more and then I promise I'll be done."

"It's like talking to a brick wall." Damien throws his hands up in frustration, stomping off to claim his place at the end of the mat, while I take mine at the top.

Taking a breath, I run down the mat, propelling myself into the move I know by heart. My body knows the number of spins and twists it takes me to hit the other side standing tall. But this time, when I hit the mat, a pain I've never felt explodes out of my foot. I fall into a heap.

"Fuck!" I shout, holding onto my leg as I curl up in pain. Shit. Shit. Shit. *Whatever this is, it can't be good.*

"What happened?" Damien is beside me in a heartbeat.

"I don't know." I try to breathe through the pain, but it's like a swift kick to the gut. Words are yelled over me, but I can't make any of them out.

"Wes. I'm going to take a look at your leg. It might hurt, but hopefully we'll be able to get it stabilized so we can get you to the clinic."

More pain radiates from my leg as the doctor moves his fingers over it. It's like a hot searing knife is carving a path down the back of my leg.

"It's likely his Achilles. Sometimes, landing on it the wrong way can rupture it."

"Fuck. How long will he be out?" Damien's harsh words are cold as they slide over me. The pain was too blinding, but as my foot is wrapped and I'm helped up, my mind goes to every possible outcome of this.

I didn't listen, and now look at me.

What if this can't be fixed?

What if I won't ever return to form?

What if I just fucked up everything I've ever been working for my entire life?

Fuck. Fuck, fuck, fuck.

"I STILL REMEMBER BEING in the hospital and being told I might never be able to dive competitively again." I'm staring into my plate, hopeful the eggs will swallow me whole as shame blankets over me. It's been awhile since I thought of that exact day. I've been living with the aftereffects for a few months now, but that day has been blacked out. "All because I felt I knew more than my coach."

"But who's to say that if you stopped that night, you might not have done it the next day? Or the day after?"

Sneaking a glance in Finn's direction, I see his eyes are soft, holding no hint of the blame that I've carried on my shoulders the last few months.

"I don't think that's quite how it works."

"It might not be," Finn says, getting up and walking over to my side of the table and sitting on the arm of my chair, "but will holding on to all this guilt make your diving any better?"

"What if I never get back to where I was?" The words

are whispered, vocalizing my greatest fear. "What if I screwed up my chance to get a gold and I'll never know what it's like to stand on a podium representing my country?"

A warm hand finds my cheek, and I turn my gaze to meet Finn's eyes. Eyes that are so easy to get lost in. "You're going to make yourself crazy playing the 'what if' game. I know my opinion might not mean much because I'm not a diver, but I think you're exactly where you're meant to be."

"What makes you say that?"

He drops a soft peck on my lips that tastes like the coffee he's been sipping on. "Because you're still training and showing your dedication to the sport. It would've been easy for you to say I'm done and walk away after everything that happened. But you didn't. You're still here, kicking ass and putting in the work every day."

"You make it sound so easy."

His thumb rubs the apple of my cheek in a soothing way. It's hard to turn away from this man. In just a short time, he's become one of the most important people in my life.

"You're the one that's doing the hard work. I just have to watch you work out and write my articles."

"Then train with me. I know we've been joking about it, but why not see if you have what it takes?"

Finn pulls back, an incredulous look on his face. "You're serious?"

"Yes. You've been watching from the sidelines this entire time. Why not see what an average day is like?" I know my eyes are gleaming with excitement.

"But I don't know the first thing about diving." Finn's face is pale, doing his best to talk himself out of this.

"Yes. But think of how great it will be as an article. The journalist stepping into the shoes of a diver for a day."

His Adam's apple bobs as his mouth opens and closes. He looks like a gaping fish.

"And I promise you I won't make you go off the ten-meter."

Finn sighs, the resignation evident. "I hate that you're using my story against me because I can't think of a good reason to say no. You don't fight fair."

"No one ever said I did."

Even Athletes Make Mistakes
By Finn Anderson

So often in professional sports, fans and observers see what went wrong and expound on how we could have changed it. In a loss, a coach often takes full responsibility and stands by their decisions, even if those decisions cost them the game.

At other times, one team member will bear the brunt of the loss, even if it's not their cross to bear.

So when Wes Cooper admitted to making a mistake, it was refreshing. After an injury sidelined his training for the next Olympic Games, Cooper openly admitted to making a mistake.

"I pushed myself too hard. I did too much in the name of training and it cost me," Cooper says.

The cost? An Achilles rupture that took away any off-season training gains he might have made. Athletes use their off-season to level up. To find the latest and greatest technique that can help them get an advantage on their opponent.

In a solitary event like diving, athletes rely on their own strength to propel them forward in a sport where only your best is good enough.

"Instead of working on leveling up, I'm back to building up basic strength in my leg. Physical therapy helped get me back to being able to walk without pain, but I'm working harder than ever before to get back to where I was. I have to build up the strength that I previously took for granted."

So how does one recover from a mistake that could have had life-altering implications?

"One day at a time," Cooper states. "I don't need to look any further ahead. I know what my ultimate goal is."

And that ultimate goal? The Olympics.

With qualifiers only a few months away, the pressure is on to be in peak physical shape. Because if Cooper doesn't make it past that stage, the Olympics will continue to be only a dream.

Chapter Fifteen

FINN

"I feel like I'm going to be the one picked last to be on the team."

Looking around the training room, I know I don't stack up against these professional athletes.

"Relax. You'll be fine. I'll go easy on you." Wes gives me a wink as he pushes me toward the weight room.

"And that worries me. I've seen how you train."

I've been here most days since this assignment started a few weeks ago. Never have I seen people train so hard. The intensity in the gym is palpable every time I'm here.

"If it makes you feel better, I'll start you off with light weights."

"Oh, so one-hundred-pound weights instead of two-hundred?" I can't hide the fear that laces my tone. If it weren't for his cute, still sleep-lined face, it would've been easier to say no to him. But as it stands, Wes is very hard to say no to.

"I was thinking more like ten-pound weights to start, but if you want to try and bench press me, I'll let you give it a shot." I'd kiss away the smirk on his face if it wouldn't lead to dragging him down on the ground and having my way with him. Ever since Vancouver, my body has been itching to be with him again. I've never felt this way before—this intense desire to be around someone all the time, even though I'm already around him most of the day. It's the nights I crave.

"You still with me?" Wes is standing in front of me, his shirt gone as he holds two weights down at his side.

"Don't take it easy on me." I hold out both hands, waiting to start.

His brow quirks up. "I know you like it rough, but maybe taking it easy might be good. I've got a lot in store for you today."

And with that, he drops two weights in my hands, and I know I'm a goner before they drop to the mat.

———

"NOW IT'S TIME TO DIVE."

I'm bent over, resting my hands on my knees, trying to suck in as much air as I can. I never truly understood how much effort goes into training. These athletes make it look easy.

"If you so much as think of getting me on that ten-meter, I will push you off without a second thought."

Wes's hand rests on my back, his lips right by my ear. Even the slightest contact has my tired body responding to him. "You do know that's not really a threat, right?"

I turn, ever so slightly, to face him. "Still. I'm not going up there."

Even the mere thought of going that high causes nerves to pebble my skin. I don't do heights.

"We won't; I promised you. But I'm making you get on

the springboards. Those are so easy, a baby could do them."

The cockiness in his tone is almost a challenge. I want to be able to do these things that Wes does, if only so I can better understand him.

"Let's do it."

I straighten, following Wes out to the pool deck. Most of the divers have gone home for the day, getting their workouts in early. Thank God. It'll be less humiliating this way.

"I'll start you off easy." Wes jumps onto the board with all the confidence in the world, like he was born to be a diver. He walks down the board, before pushing up off his toes and diving gracefully into the water.

He exudes power as he pops out of the water. It's like the first time I met him. The water clings to him like it needs him to survive. Like nothing is immune to the charm and influence of Wes Cooper.

"See something you like?" Wes comes to stand toe-to-toe with me. Rivulets run down his chest, causing me to lick my lips.

"You know I do." I run a single finger down the valley of Wes's chest. Goose bumps erupt in my path. I love that I have this effect on him. I don't kid myself. I don't look anything like the people he used to hook up with. I'm tall and lanky, without a shred of muscle. Wes is the sexiest man I've ever met. With that smile and those dimples, he could have any man he wants. And yet, here he is, grabbing my hand and kissing my wrist. The warm contact of his lips has my blood surging.

"I can't say the view is all that bad from where I'm standing."

"You know," I step closer to Wes, letting my free hand

rest on his chest, "we could get a better view of each other somewhere else."

Heat swirls in Wes's eyes. I've got him right where I want him. His lips brush against my jaw, making their way to my ear. "If you're trying to distract me, you need to try harder."

And then he's gone. I lament the loss of him as I look around, trying to break through the lustful spell he put me under. Wes is leaning against the ladder of the board, crooking a finger to beckon me forward. "Get up there and let's see what you've got."

I grumble as I make my way over to him. A smack to the ass has me hurrying along.

"If you keep stalling, I'll make you get up on the five-meter."

"I'm going, I'm going." Walking to the end of the board, I do my best to remember everything I learned during swimming lessons when I was a kid. Swimming was never my favorite, but I try to muster everything I know so I don't embarrass myself in front of Wes.

Taking a deep breath, I extend my arms overhead and push off the board. The spring is more sensitive than I anticipate, and it catches my foot as I belly flop into the pool.

Unprepared, I suck in a mouthful of water, coming up sputtering and coughing like an idiot.

"You okay?" Wes asks from where he now sits on the edge of the pool, no trace of playfulness in his voice.

"Mostly my pride has taken a hit." I swim over to him, resting my arms on the side of the pool. My body is gassed from the earlier workout. "How'd you learn to dive like you did?"

"Doing exactly what you just did." Wes gazes down at me with a sympathetic look in his eye. "I didn't just start jumping off the ten-meter, knowing everything there is to know about diving."

"You make it look so easy." I push up out of the water, sitting next to Wes.

"Trust me, it's not. I'm not even going to have you attempt tumbling. Because doing that from thirty feet in the air, while worrying about your form and what the judges will see if even a toe is out of line, is enough to make you go crazy."

"How does the pressure not get to you?"

Wes's face pinches in response. "It does in little ways. Pushing myself too hard. Not going out with friends. Sacrificing a social life in order to be the best diver I can be. It's so close, I can almost taste it."

"What happens if you don't get it?" I blurt the question out before thinking.

Wes stands, walking back over to the board. Shit. Sometimes my mouth gets me in trouble. Wes is pacing now, and I don't make a move to go to him. Something is off.

"I try not to think about it too much." His hand is resting on the one-meter board, eyes focused on that point. "Because if I focus on that, then why would I want to train as hard as I do?"

The wistfulness in his tone cuts deep. He's trying to play it off, but I know I struck a chord.

"I've got another twelve months until I find out. No sense in worrying until then, right?"

If only I believed him. Wes has seemed nothing but sure of himself since I've met him. This tentative side to him is something I'm not familiar with. It feels like the ground is shifting beneath us, and I don't know where I stand with him.

"You ready to try again?" Wes's mask is back on, fixed

firmly over the emotions that were trying to creep out of him. If I didn't feel so bad for pulling back the veil, I'd poke him. But instead, I plaster on a fake smile and try to muster up all the courage I can.

"As ready as I'll ever be." I shrug, standing and walking over to him.

"Then how about the ten-meter?"

I push him out of the way, walking down the spring-board. "I'll let you know when I have a death wish."

Jumping into the water, my arms smack the pool before sinking under. Wes is waiting by the side, ready to give instruction.

"Don't let your arms go out to the side. Smacking the water from the high boards is painful."

"Not as painful as this. My hair hurts. Is that possible?" My breaths are labored, trying to suck in as much air as possible.

"It can't be that bad." Wes's handsome face appears over mine, as I rest my arms on the side of the pool.

"I don't think I can move. Do you always feel like this when you're done?" I pant, the pool causing my already weak muscles to go into overdrive to get me to the side. Muscles I didn't even know I had hurt. And not in a good way.

"If I push too hard, I hurt, but not like this. Need me to make it better?" The playful lilt to his tone does little to perk me up.

"That depends. Do you have a time machine so I can go back in time and not agree to this asinine decision?"

Wes sticks his hand down, helping me out of the pool. I wish we were both wet and sweaty for different reasons, but I'm not that lucky today.

"Does it make you appreciate what I do?" Wes and I

are standing chest to chest, and it takes everything I have not to drop all my weight onto him.

"It makes me appreciate the fact that there's no way I could ever do what you do.

WES

WHAT HAPPENS *if you don't get it?*

That question has been rolling around in my brain with nowhere to go. I know it was an innocent question, one Finn would take back if he could. I saw it the minute he asked it, the regret etched on his face. But he can't.

And I can't stop thinking about that question. The qualifiers seem to be getting closer and closer, like a speeding freight train about to crash.

But all I think about is what's going to happen after. What happens if I put in all this work to rehab and train and I don't win? It's everything I've been working toward since I started diving.

Failure sits like an anvil, heavy on my chest, pressing further into me. Instead of bringing Finn back to my place, I kissed him and sent him on his way, claiming training would come early tomorrow and there'd be no time for fun.

But really, I didn't want him to see me sitting up and thinking about those words he said. Ever since Finn has come into my life, it's put a spotlight on things I haven't given much thought to.

I think it's something every athlete grapples with. What happens when all your hard work is for naught? When the one thing that is your sole focus in life is no longer there?

When you're too old and washed up, and you're forced out before you're ready?

Olympic diving has been my entire life since I was fourteen. I don't remember my life without it. My formative years were spent being carted to and from the pool by my mom in the early morning hours and after school. It wasn't just my entire life, but my parents' too. It feels like if I don't win, I'll be letting them down.

It's always been at the back of my mind—what would happen if I never won. But it was something I managed not to think about. And now, Finn comes blowing into my life and is asking the hard questions.

He has managed to rock my entire world. Not just my professional life, but my personal one as well. I've never wanted to make time for another person before. I was fine with the casual hookups that were meaningless—a way to get off when I needed a release.

But not with Finn. Finn is the most unexpected thing that has ever happened to me. My life was fine. Great, even. Then Finn came and turned everything on its head. Never have I wanted to be with a person more. I find myself wanting to leave the pool just so we can spend time together. Even though we're around each other all day, every day, I'm not sick of him.

I crave this man with a need I've never known. His mind. His body. That smile that manages to light my body on fire and leave me in a pile of ash. All I want is Finn, the journalist who is writing my story in a way I never knew needed to be told. I didn't want to fall for him, but life is funny that way.

Don't Quit Your Day Job
By Finn Anderson

We've all been there. We're watching the game and saying how we can do better than the athlete performing. Whether it's football, baseball, or curling, we all think we can do it.

We armchair athletes think we can do better than the professionals. But I'm here to tell you we're wrong. We cannot outperform these athletes who have been training their entire lives in the name of their sport.

As someone with little-to-no athletic talent, I spent a day training with Olympian Wes Cooper, and it gave me a whole new appreciation for the dedication these athletes have to their craft. Not once did he whine about the endless weights or dry land training he was doing, sometimes over and over again.

"I've dedicated myself to this sport for over thirteen years. I know what's expected and what I have to do to be in peak shape to compete," Cooper says. "It's second nature to me now."

Mirroring Cooper's own schedule, I was awake before the sun came up, at the gym earlier than most people get out of bed, and trying to do complicated twisting moves that mimic the dives he performs.

After two rounds in the weight room I was ready to throw in the towel. And that was only half of the day.

What these athletes do is not easy. I used muscles I didn't even know I had. Even my hair hurt.

So next time you think about yelling at the TV about how you could do a better job? Take a minute to think about everything that went into that moment. About the athlete's never-ending dedication to the sport. Watching what they eat and drink every day. Pushing themselves to and sometimes past their breaking point.

Did you really think about it? Yeah?

Don't quit your day job.

107

Chapter Sixteen

WES

"I'm so sorry I didn't call you." Finn pulls open the front door of his sister's house, a frown on his face.

"What's wrong?" A crash sounds from somewhere deep in the house.

"Mel got stuck at work. Big accident, so all hands on deck. And my parents couldn't babysit, so…" Finn shuts the door behind me, racing off to find the source of the noise.

Toeing off my shoes, I follow him through the open living room into the kitchen. Puffs of flour are settling over every space that's visible. A little girl looks like a ghost next to him.

"I told you I would help with this part." Finn waves a hand through the air, trying to get some of the offending flour to settle.

"Sorry, Uncle Finn." She looks properly chastised when she sees me. "Who's that?"

"Darcy, that is Wes. Wes, this is my niece, Darcy."

"Hi, Darcy." I give a hesitant wave in her direction.

"Are you here to help us bake?"

"I guess I am." I shuffle into the kitchen. Finn is covered in a fine layer of white particles, his eyes hard to see through his covered glasses. "Can I help with anything?"

"We need more flour!" Darcy pipes up.

"Let one of us do it. We already have a huge mess to clean up." Finn blows out a breath, disturbing the flour that clings to him like a second skin.

"You're kind of hard to take seriously when you look like that." I don't fight the smile that pulls at my mouth. Darcy waggles a finger, pulling my attention down to her.

"He's easy when you know what to do. I have him wrapped around my finger," Darcy whispers in my ear, covering her mouth so Finn can't hear. I hold back my laugh.

"What are you two whispering about over there?"

"Oh nothing." Darcy gives me a mischievous look before running off to the other side of the island. "Can I start cleaning?" Pushing up my sleeves, I rest my hands on my hips, facing the chaos.

Finn blows out an exasperated breath. "Get me a new kitchen?"

"Nice try. What are we making?"

"I wanted to make cupcakes for Mom when she gets home. They make her happy," Darcy explained.

"They do. But next time, wait for me to help measure." Finn drops a kiss on her forehead before facing me. "Want to help measure the dry ingredients?"

I nod, stepping next to Finn and getting to work. Darcy sings to herself as she stirs the wet ingredients around. "It's nice that you do things like this with your niece." My voice is quiet as I measure ingredients into a bright pink mixing bowl.

"I live here rent free. It's the least I could do. I'm just sad we won't make the movie tonight."

I shrug my shoulders. "If I'm being honest, this is probably a lot better."

"Yeah?" Finn shoves his glasses farther up his nose. "You're not upset?"

"While there are some advantages to dark rooms, I'd much rather actually get to spend time with you."

Finn bursts out in laughter, shocking Darcy next to him. "You realize we spend all day together, right?"

Taking the bowl from me, Finn dumps the ingredients into the mixer. Darcy is waiting eagerly to start mixing. "I know. But most of the time you're writing, and I'm working out or in the pool."

Finn rolls his eyes, flour still coating his thick eyebrows. "Such a hardship for me. Getting to watch you strut around in a Speedo all day."

"What's a Speedo?" Darcy's curious voice asks.

"It's a swimsuit," Finn answers quickly. Pink stains his cheeks at the question. "Keep mixing and then we'll spoon the batter into the cupcake tin."

Finn shoves at my chest, pushing me toward the sink, away from open ears. "I like seeing you like this. All hot and bothered."

"Stop it." Finn points a wet spatula in my face as my smile grows.

"What? Just saying I like teasing my boyfriend. What's so wrong with that?"

The spatula clatters to the countertop. "Boyfriend?" His voice cracks as the single word leaves him.

Oh shit. I didn't even realize I said it. The panicked look on his face has me wanting to backtrack, but Darcy cuts us off. "Ready to go, Uncle Finn!"

Finn's mouth is open, gaping at me like I just proposed

marriage. Spinning around, Finn goes to help Darcy pour out the batter before putting the trays in the oven. But my mind is still reeling.

I don't think I've ever called anyone my boyfriend before. I've had a few flings here and there that might have lasted longer than a month, but nothing serious. And Finn and I haven't even been together that long. The word feels heavy, rolling around in my brain like it's going to come after the two of us.

But it also feels right. I balked at the idea of having a reporter following me around. I didn't want to show any weakness and give anyone any reason to doubt me. I know I'm ready to be back, even if it's hard some days, but I didn't want to become fodder for the tabloids.

Finn has never given me any doubt. He's never made me feel cheap or that I was merely a means to get ahead for him. The thought of being in a relationship with anyone used to make me run scared in the other direction.

But the only direction I want to be running in is Finn's. When he's watching me at practice, I want to perform better. I make sure my rip entries are smaller so he'll be impressed. I know a lot of it doesn't mean much to Finn, who is adorably clueless about sports, but I want him to be proud of me.

"Can we watch a movie while we wait for the cupcakes?" Darcy's eager voice breaks me from my thoughts.

"Sure. Go put on your pajamas and then you can pick one to watch."

"Looks like we're getting our movie after all," I joke, trying to cut the tension coming off Finn in waves.

"Probably not the same kind of movie we were going to see, but I suppose so. Maybe we could have our own sleepover later."

Pushing off the counter behind me, I move around the large kitchen, caging Finn in where he stands. "You know I wish we could, but training always comes early."

Finn lets out a sigh. "I know."

I hate the tone of disappointment in his voice. But as the games loom closer, the nights get longer. I can't seem to sleep well, staying up and worrying about everything that might or might not happen. I don't want to worry Finn.

"Are you sure you'd even want me to stay? You looked pretty freaked out after I called you my boyfriend."

He doesn't say anything, but the slight tic in his jaw tells me yes. "I just…wasn't expecting it."

"I mean, if you're not my boyfriend, then what are we?" I wave a finger between us. "If you want this to be casual, that's fine." I take a step back, but Finn locks a hand around my waist and pulls me back. We've had a few sleepovers, so it's more than casual to me.

"No. I don't want to be casual. Casual means you can see other people, and I don't want you seeing other people."

"But you don't want me calling you my boyfriend?" I quirk a brow up. Finn drops his head to my shoulder.

"Are you always this insufferable?"

Wrapping my arms around him, I pull him in closer, loving the feel of his lithe body against mine. "Only around you, I'm afraid," I whisper against his neck.

Finn pulls back, his deep brown eyes locking with my own. "Do I want you to be my boyfriend? Yes. But I'm scared."

"Why are you scared?" There's not an ounce of humor in my voice as I study Finn's face. Usually so open, it's hard to get a read on what he's feeling.

"That it won't last. That I'm convenient for you because we're around each other all the time. Once I'm done with this whole piece on you, where does that leave us? I don't want to be tossed out—"

I cut him off with a soft kiss to his lips. I swallow the gasp of shock as his hands fist in my shirt, keeping me locked to him. I don't make a move to deepen the kiss, aware that small eyes will be back here any minute. But I want Finn to know what I'm feeling right now.

"Is that really what you think?" I whisper against his lips. "That I'm going to toss you out once the stories on me have dried up?"

Finn drops his eyes, not looking at me. "My college boyfriend dropped me for a lot less. Said I wouldn't fit in with his postcollege lifestyle in New York, and that was the last I saw of him."

My molars grind in anger at the person who could be so careless with this man in front of me. "That's his loss." Cupping his chin, I bring his gaze to meet mine. I want him to feel the words as I say them. "You are not something to be tossed aside. Even if you're not ready for it, I want you to be my boyfriend. You're the first person who has made me want to even have one. You're unlike anyone I've ever met. You see the real me, not just the diver. I don't have to put on a front for you, and it makes it easy to be around you."

"Would it make you feel better if I told you I didn't know who you were when I got this assignment?" Finn traces a finger over my brow, as if memorizing the detail.

"I'd say I am shocked, but I'd be lying."

"Sorry I don't know all the sports things, but at least I'm trying to learn."

I drop a soft kiss onto his lips, needing to feel him. "You are a very good learner, Finn."

"What can I say? You make it easy."

Chapter Seventeen

WES

"So there's a slight change of plans," I say when I meet Finn at the end of the driveway as he steps out of his car. We rescheduled our date night, and once again, fate had other plans.

"Why is this becoming our normal?" The late evening light casts his eyes in a heavenly glow. God, could this man be any sexier? It has me almost forgetting why I'm meeting him out here.

"Because my mom decided to come into town to check on me today and is now making us dinner?" My voice rises, like I'm questioning what's actually happening.

"Your mom is here?" Finn practically shouts. "Like your mom mom? The lady who gave birth to you and raised you is here in your house?"

"Yes?" Again, it comes out as a question. I don't know why I'm so worried about her meeting Finn. Maybe because he's the first person I've cared about and actually want to stick around. Or maybe it's because when I called him my boyfriend last week he panicked.

"A heads-up might've been nice. I don't think I look nice enough to meet your mom." I step back from him, trailing my eyes over his dark, fitted jeans, white button-down that's neatly tucked in, and his tan jacket.

"I don't think you could look any more perfect to meet her. She'll eat you up." I lean in, pressing a soft kiss to his lips. Lemon. I go back in, taking another drink of his lips, not wanting to leave this moment and go inside. I can feel the second Finn's brain shuts off from the spiral he was in, melting into me and resting his hands on my stomach. It sets up a tidal wave of pressure there, building until I'm pushing him back against his car.

"As much as I would like to continue doing this," Finn says as he breaks the kiss, and I trail my lips down his jaw, "your mom is probably wondering where we are. I'd hate for her to think I'm a bad influence on you."

I huff out a laugh as I rest my head in the crook of his neck, inhaling his clean scent. "I don't think that's possible. You look like a Boy Scout."

Finn pushes me off of him, threading his fingers with mine. "C'mon. If I'm going to meet your mom, we might as well get it over with."

"Okay, she's not that bad." I squeeze his hand as we make our way up the sidewalk. Low-hanging ivy casts long shadows across the yard.

"Yes, but I'm not prepared. You know how I can be."

"I do, and I know you have nothing to worry about."

Pushing open the door, the heavenly scents of garlic and marinara waft our way.

"Where'd you go, dear?" My mom pops her head around the corner. "Oh, is this the Finn I've been hearing so much about?" She pats her graying, pixie-cut hair down as she comes into the entryway.

I nod. "Mom, this is Finn…" My boyfriend? The journalist who is following me around for the next however many months and whom I'm fucking every chance I can get?

"His boyfriend." My neck cracks from how fast my gaze swings to him. Instead of showing the panic that the word brought before, he's steady. Strong. Like he's had time to mull it over and decide that's what we are, even if I've known it for a lot longer. And the smile that lights up his face? It does swirly things to my insides that I'm not used to feeling but that I'm beginning to like feeling with Finn.

"My boyfriend." My smile matches his.

"It's nice to meet you, Mrs. Cooper." Finn extends his hand, but my mom swats it away, pulling him down to her in a hug only a mom can give.

"We hug here, Finn. Call me Mary. It's so nice to finally meet a boyfriend of Wes's." She pulls back, resting her hands on his face as she looks at him. "You look like such a nice boy."

"Oh God, Mom." I rub my hand over my eyes, wishing a sinkhole would swallow me whole right now.

"What? He does." She drops her hands, moving into the kitchen. "You're staying for dinner? I'm making my famous spaghetti Bolognese. Wessy has always loved it."

Wessy? Finn mouths, turning to follow my mom into the kitchen. "Spaghetti sounds wonderful, Mary. How can I help?"

And just like that, Finn endears himself to my mother.

Finn

"Would you please stop with the stories?" Wes groans as he eyes the wine in my hand. In true Wes fashion, he hasn't had a drop. His body is a temple, one I love worshipping. And he treats it that way.

"Please don't. I want to hear more." My eyes are sparkling as I sip my wine, enjoying the cool air the late summer night is bringing. The lights hanging over the backyard give everything an ethereal glow.

I'm finding the more time I spend with Wes, the more magical everything becomes. It's cheesy, I know. But it's been a long time since I've felt like this.

"There was the one time that he got caught skinny-dipping in the pool. His friends bet him he wouldn't dive naked. If they knew anything about him, they would've known that he would do it. His friends' parents came home early and it was a whole ordeal." Mary is cackling with laughter, having drank most of the wine from the bottle we opened.

Wes's face is as red as the sauce that lingers on the empty plates in front of us. "This is horrifying. It's getting late. Mom, you should go to bed." Standing to clear the plates, Wes tries to shoo his mother inside.

"Oh, what's a few more embarrassing stories? I'm enjoying getting to know Finn. I can't remember the last time you brought a boy home."

"Oh, this I'm definitely interested in." I scooch closer, propping my hand on the table and resting my chin in my hand. "How many boyfriends did Wes have?"

"I think you're both done now." Wes stalks off to the house, taking the wine with him.

"Oh sweetheart, I haven't met anyone Wes has dated in years."

"Years?"

"Wes's lifestyle certainly isn't the most stable. No one has ever wanted to stick around for him." Her voice takes on a sad tone, one that hits me square in the chest.

Sipping my wine, I look back to the house. The patio doors give me a glimpse of Wes in the kitchen, scrubbing everything down.

"It's certainly different."

"I'd ask you your intentions with my son, but it seems pretty clear to me."

My head whips around to look at her. "It does?"

Mary's cheeks are glowing from the wine we've had. "You two are smitten with each other."

A blush crawls up my neck, hot and thick. "It's still new. I wouldn't want to do anything to take Wes's focus away from diving."

"But that's what he needs. Bless that sweet boy in there, but he needs to learn there's more to life than diving."

I hate to agree with her, but she does have a point. Since I've met Wes, his focus has been singularly on diving. On making sure he's ready to be at the top of his game to make the Olympics. I cherish the few nights we get together, because I know anything more than a night or two out is too much for Wes and his religious training schedule.

"He's too stubborn to let anything take his focus away from diving."

"Stubborn, yes. But he just hasn't found the right person to make him put in the effort to do so. But it seems like he might have found that with you."

What is it with moms dropping nuggets of truth when you least expect them?

"Everything going okay out here?" Wes appears behind me, settling his hands on my shoulders.

Mary slaps her hands on her knees, standing abruptly

from the table. "I think it's time I called it a night. I hope you come to the cookout I'm planning for the team tomorrow."

"Cookout?" Wes questions.

"Yes. Did you think I'd come into town and not see the team? I've already let Damien know. Now, don't stay up too late." She pats Wes on the cheek as she comes around the table. "And it was lovely to meet you, Finn."

Wes waits until the soft click of the door shuts behind her. "Was she terrible?" He drops down into my lap, wrapping his arms around my shoulders.

"Not at all. I can see where you get your passion for life."

"That's what you got from meeting her?" Wes's eyes are playful as he looks down at me.

"Aside from amazing stories about you growing up, yeah. She's great. I'm glad our plans keep getting waylaid. Means I get to learn more about you." I brush a lock of hair that falls into his eyes.

"What haven't you learned about me yet? You're with me all the time."

"You say that like it's a bad thing." I drag a finger down Wes's chest, his body shuddering beneath my touch.

"It's just…" Wes sighs. "I've gotten used to having you around. What happens when your assignment is over?"

"Then we date like normal people. You have done that before, right?"

"This wine has made you loose-lipped tonight."

I squeeze his thigh, bringing his attention back to me. "Just stating a truth. I know I might have freaked out on you last week when you called me your boyfriend, but that's what we are."

Wes runs his knuckles over my cheek and I lean into his

touch, craving the warmth that spreads through me. "You're not freaking out about it?"

I shake my head. "No. So whatever has your brain worrying about the future, stop. You're not going to get rid of me that easily."

Wes leans in for an eager, hungry kiss. "Good."

Chapter Eighteen

FINN

Knocking on the door, I take a deep breath, trying to calm my nerves. It's not like I haven't hung out with Wes and his teammates before. But something about being around them in this relaxed setting has me on edge.

Almost like I have to impress them for me to get Wes's seal of approval. I know, it's dumb, but I can't help it. I want them to like me because I want to stick around.

"You made it." Wes's beaming smile greets me, making me weak in the knees.

"Here. I brought cupcakes." I shove them at him like a crazy person might.

"Thanks," he says on a laugh. "Everyone's out back."

Following Wes through the kitchen, I can hear the voices from his teammates in the backyard. My nerves ratchet up before I can tell myself that'll it be okay.

"Hey! Finn is here!" Simone calls, running over to wrap me in a hug.

"Hey. Hi." I wave awkwardly at her, silently chastising myself.

"I'm so happy you could make it. Wes has been talking about you all day."

"Really?" My gaze swings to find him opening a water bottle next to his mom.

"Oh yes, dear. He was very excited," Mary whispers, wrapping her arms around me for a mom hug.

"Try to make me sound less cool, please." Wes rolls his eyes at everyone.

"I'm sure your mom could tell another story or two if you really wanted." I waggle my eyes at Wes as his mom heads over to the grill.

"Okay, that's enough bonding time. I like you being around, and I don't want my mom to scare you off. Come help me start the fire."

"You're no fun," Simone laughs. "Go help your mom. Dan and I will help Finn."

Wes gives me a disgruntled look before going over to help his mom. "You know he thinks you're going to tell me stories about him now, don't you?"

Simone shrugs, throwing a few logs into the firepit. "Eh, let him think that." Simone peeks over her shoulder, before focusing her green eyes on me. It takes everything I have not to wither under her stare.

"You're good for him, you know."

"How do you mean?" I grab the lighter and starter, helping to get the fire going.

"I mean, I don't think I've ever seen him do something like this in the middle of the season."

"Wasn't it his mom who organized this?" I wave my hand around the backyard. "She was the one who invited me."

"True, but usually after training, Wes would just come home and hole up here and we wouldn't see him." Dan says it so matter-of-factly with no room for argument.

"You make him smile. We like that." Simone smiles back at me, like she's happy with me doing it.

"When I first came, everyone warned me that if Wes was cranky to tell them and they'd straighten him out for me. I think we have very different ideas of what Wes is really like."

Simone and Dan each burst out laughing. "That's because you're sleeping with him. Everyone is different around the person they like."

The blush creeps up my cheeks unbidden. "Are we that obvious?" I adjust my glasses, trying to fight the nerves.

"Not really," Simone says, shrugging a shoulder as she passes me a beer. "But Wes seems happier, and it started when you came around. We can put two and two together."

"I mean, you both also left the poker game pretty quickly in Vancouver," Dan laughs, taking a sip of his own drink. Simone elbows him in the gut.

"We weren't going to mention that," she hisses. "Anyway, just know that we like the two of you together."

Simone winks at me, as they both go to greet the newest arrival who just walked out back. I stay where I am, observing everyone. I like that this is a close-knit group. And that Simone and Dan easily welcomed me in as if I've always been a part of it.

"Sorry I was gone for so long. The grilling took longer than I thought it would." Wes throws an arm around my shoulders as he comes over to stand next to me. "Doing okay?"

I nod, sipping at my beer. "I think so."

"You think so? They didn't scare you off, did they?"

I shrug my shoulders, picking at the sodden label sticking to the glass. "No. Although, they do know about us." I wave the bottle in my hand between the two of us. "Apparently we're not as subtle as we think."

"Were we trying to be? Because I think I've made it pretty clear how I feel about you."

"Oh yeah? And how's that?" I'm fishing. I know it.

"That I like you, a lot, and that I want to see where this goes between us."

"Really?"

"Why does that surprise you?" Wes asks, sitting in one of the seats around the now blazing fire. He pulls me down to the seat next to him, turning to give me his full attention. Everyone else is scattered around the yard, playing games or talking, paying us no attention. "I called you my boyfriend, and even though you were playing catch up, I want to see where this thing goes."

I grab his hand, holding it in my own. "Your life is crazy. You have trainings around the world, competitions, photoshoots. I'm a small-town reporter who doesn't know where he'll be in the next few years. Even if our lives are on two different trajectories, I want you."

"Has anyone ever told you that you think too much?" Wes smooths out the line that has no doubt appeared between my eyebrows.

"I may have heard it once or twice."

"I live a crazy life, there's no denying it. But if something is right, it'll work out."

"You have a lot of confidence."

Wes shrugs a shoulder. "Eh, so I've been told. But it's not confidence, Finn."

"No?" I quirk a brow in his direction. The light of the moon casts him in a golden halo. The sight of him takes my breath away.

"No. I know a good thing when I see it. And Finn?"

I gulp, leaning closer, my throat dry as his words infil-
trate every sense of who I am and take over. Wes's hand
pulls me farther into his bubble. His eyes are ablaze with
heat.

"This is a very good thing."

Chapter Nineteen

WES

Seeing the look in Finn's eyes, I don't want to be anywhere other than with him. Just the two of us. Grabbing his hand, I lead him around the side of my house to my private patio door.

"Don't you have guests to entertain?" His whispered words send heat throughout my body.

"Technically, my mom invited them. They can make do without us for now." I don't care if anyone saw us slip away. I just need to be with Finn.

Pulling the door open, I guide Finn in behind me, shutting the door and closing the curtains for privacy.

I press Finn up against the wall, settling my hips in the cradle of his. His hard cock against mine is heaven and hell. So close, but still too much between us.

"Good. Because I need you right now," Finn announces.

I attack his lips with a fervor I've never felt. My body aches for Finn. It yearns for him in every way. I can't get enough of this feeling as our tongues tangle and fight for control.

Finn pushes off the wall, his hands wrapping around me as he walks us toward my bed. "Fuck, Wes." He drops his forehead to mine as I sink onto the soft duvet behind me. I'm dizzy with need and anticipation.

Pulling my shirt off, I throw it behind me and lie down, pulling Finn on top of me. He straddles my hips, rocking into me.

"You are so sexy when you're turned on." Finn runs a finger down my chest, lust settling in my groin.

"Are you going to do something about it?" I thrust my hips, searching for any kind of relief.

Finn leans over me, the soft cotton of his shirt brushing against my chest. "Maybe I want to take my time."

His lips ghost mine, brushing lightly as he moves his way down my body. "I want to worship and savor you." His hot breath has chills spreading throughout my body. "You deserve to be adored."

My heart stutters in my chest, reveling in his words as he unbuttons my jeans and slides them down my legs. I don't know when he flipped the script, but I like it.

He's slow on his way back up, kissing his way up my leg. My dick is demanding attention, trying to punch through my boxer briefs. Finn is making me crazy, not moving fast enough.

I move my hand over my aching cock, but Finn smacks my hand away. "Oh no. That's all for me tonight."

"Then what's taking you so long?" I thrust up again, trying to bring him where I want him most.

"Patience, Wes. Patience."

His lips are warm as they suck and nibble on the tender skin of my hips. He's all tease, not moving any lower. A growl escapes my lips.

"Someone is needy tonight."

Finn licks a trail up my stomach, blowing lightly on it.

"It's because I need you." I reach down, bringing him up and capturing his lips with mine. I'm greedy, taking what he isn't giving me. Wrapping my legs around his hips, I flip us over, grinding down over him. I could easily get off like this, but I want to be inside of Finn for that.

Pushing his shirt up, I kiss my way down his abs. If I weren't mad with need, I'd take my time. His abs are made to be worshipped with my tongue. But for now, I strip off his pants and boxers and take his heavy cock in hand.

"You're not wasting any time," he hisses.

"Someone drove me crazy," I say before dragging my tongue along the throbbing vein on the underside of his dick. Swirling the sticky precum around the head, I take him as far back as I can go. Finn's head is thrown back in pleasure as I reach into my own briefs and take my cock in hand.

Seeing Finn become unraveled at my touch has me ready to come undone. He thrusts up, hitting the back of my throat as I continue bobbing up and down his hard length. I sneak a hand down, playing with his balls.

"No. Stop." Finn's words are pained as he pulls me off of him. "I'm going to come if you keep doing that."

"What if I want you to come down my throat?" My voice is gravelly, coated with need as I pull off him, dragging my hand up and down his cock.

"I want you to come inside me." Finn pulls me up him, sticking his hands in the back of my briefs and squeezing my ass.

"Grab the lube." My voice is demanding as he stretches behind, grabbing the bottle from my nightstand along with a condom.

Snapping the bottle open, I coat my fingers and hover over him. One of his hands snakes around my back, pulling me closer to him as he pulls my boxers off me. The heated look in his eyes could spark a fire.

I find his lips as my fingers press against his ass, pushing inside. Finn sinks down on them, welcoming the intrusion.

"God, you feel amazing, Wes." He bucks against me as my lips seek his. Our breaths mingle as I add another finger. My hand finds our cocks, leaking against his stomach, as we both thrust through my fist. We're both hard with need, dripping.

"I'm ready. Please, Wes."

I can't wait another minute. If I'm not inside him, I'm going to explode. Grabbing the condom, Finn rolls it down and guides me to his rim before I ease inside. He hisses, not fully prepped.

"You okay?" I run my hand down his chest, snaking my hand around his back and pulling him to me, so impossibly close to me. Not a piece of paper could fit between us. Our hearts beat together as we hold one another. The moment is bigger than a needy fuck between the two of us. It's more. And from the look in Finn's eyes, I know he feels it too.

"Yes," Finn replies, and I kiss him as I start to move. My tongue matches each thrust, each drive, as I move inside him. I know every time I hit that spot deep inside him. My balls draw up tighter, needing to come but wanting to draw out my pleasure just a bit longer.

I move my hands, resting one over his heart. It's a rapid beat against his ribs as he fights to keep control.

"Let go," I whisper. Dropping my forehead to Finn, I drive harder and harder into him, as I lose it. I don't have to touch Finn as he starts to pulse and come on his stomach.

"Fuck," I growl out as he holds me to him and I start to

come. Each pulse inside the condom drags my release out that much longer.

Our breaths mingle together. We're a hot, sweaty, sticky mess, but neither of us makes any move to get up.

Finn flips onto his side, with me still lodged deep inside him. His fingers drag over my face, as if memorizing my features. I capture his hand, holding it to me.

It felt hurried and frenzied, but now a peace has settled over me. I have no idea what's going to happen with Finn, but right now, things feel pretty perfect.

And I could get used to this.

Chapter Twenty

FINN

"So this is really how you want to spend our date night?" Wes shuts the door, rounding the car to me, hands shoved deep into his pockets. "Now that we finally get to go out, just the two of us, we're going bowling?"

"Well, it seems everything we do you're already good at, so I'd like to see how you do when you're trying something new." I drop a brief kiss on his lips and turn toward the bowling alley.

Wes shuffles in as I hold the door open, taking in his unsure posture. The entire time we've been together, he's been successful at everything he does. He's a perfectionist; I can't fault him for that. He trains for perfection.

"Hey, Finn. How ya doin' tonight?" Tom, the alley owner asks.

"Good. Got a free lane?"

"For our best bowler? Sure do." I hand over my credit card as he asks Wes for his shoe size.

"Thanks, Tom." I nod at him as I lead Wes down to our lane.

"I like that they know you here," Wes says, dropping down into a seat at our lane.

"Like I said, bowling is one of the things I like doing, so I come here often."

"How often?" Wes toes off his shoes and puts on the rented pair.

"You do know how bowling works, right?" I quirk a brow at him, ignoring his question.

Wes stomps after tying his shoes, piercing me with a fierce look. "I'm not a bowler, but I'm not an idiot." Wes walks over, testing out the balls at the return.

"Make sure you find a ball that fits your fingers," I say, wiping off my own ball.

Wes turns, a grin pasted on his face. "Oh yeah?"

I nod my head, walking over to set my own ball in the return. "It'll make it easier."

Wes wraps an arm around my shoulder, pulling me into his front. His lips ghost over mine. "I happen to know some balls that fit perfectly in my *fingers*."

It takes me a minute to realize what I said. "Oh, very funny."

"I'm serious. I know where some are that will work perfectly." Wes's hand drifts down my back, but I grab it, stopping it in his tracks.

"Mr. Cooper. Are you trying to distract me?" My eyes find his. They're half lust-filled, half playful.

"What if I am, Mr. Anderson?" The way he says my name has my dick hardening in my pants.

My hands trail up his chest, appreciating the muscles hidden beneath his tight T-shirt. "Then you'll sorely regret it." I smack a loud kiss to his lips and pull away from him. Grabbing my ball, I stand at the top of the lane.

"You think watching you bend over is going to make this any easier for me?" Wes calls from behind me.

"Now you know how I feel." I swing the ball back and let it rip from my fingers, hearing it clack as it hits the wooden lane and speeds down, slamming into all ten pins.

"Yes!" I pump a fist, turning back to find a glowering Wes.

"Show off," he mumbles, walking past me.

"Go get 'em, tiger." I slap him on the ass as he takes his own ball and prepares to sail it down the lane. I watch as he makes a bad move and clips two pins.

"Nicely done." I clap. He sulks his way back to me, plopping into the seat next to me.

"How often do you do this? You never answered." Wes grabs the water sitting in front of him and takes a large gulp.

I sigh. "I'm in a league. I know, I know. You're dating someone really cool." I roll my eyes, sipping my beer.

Wes brushes a lock of hair off my forehead, leaning in closer. His cool lips find my overheated skin. Anytime he's near, my body heats with anticipation. "You're right. I am dating someone *very* cool."

I shove him, trying to push him toward the ball return.

"I'm serious." Wes grabs my hand, pulling me into him. "You don't see yourself the way I see you."

"And how is it you see me?"

Wes's hand closes over mine, his thumb rubbing over my knuckles. "I see a talented writer. Someone who is kicking ass at a project that he knows nothing about. Someone who never backs down from a challenge. I see someone who cares for me, making me wonder how I got so lucky."

"Is that all?" Heat blooms over my cheeks at his words.

"No." This time, Wes turns to face me, his forehead pressing against mine. "You're one of the sexiest men I've ever met. The way you turn me on,"—he drags a finger over the beat of my pulse in my wrist—"you don't even know what you do to me."

Shivers rack my body. "Pretty sure it's how you make me feel." My voice escapes me in a whoosh. Every day I'm with Wes is better than the last. When I received this assignment, I thought it'd be like any other. I never thought I'd meet someone like Wes. That I would find someone who makes me feel like this. But I did.

"Now, are you going to show me how this is done?" Wes's words stir me out of my reverie. "I get another turn, right?"

"Someone has to. But first." I clasp his cheeks in mine and bring him in for a kiss. A deep, long, lingering kiss.

I pull back, Wes following, seeking more. "Can we do more of this instead?" His eyes are hooded.

"Maybe later." I drop one more quick kiss, wishing I could continue in the crowded alley, before standing and following Wes.

"Here's how you do it." I stand behind him, ignoring the sparks jumping between us. I straighten his hips, bringing our joined hands up. "Now just take an easy step before bringing the ball back and releasing it."

I let him go and watch as Wes follows my instructions, the ball sailing perfectly down the alley and knocking down the remainder of the pins.

"Holy shit!" Wes jumps up, before he leaps into my arms. My very unprepared arms, as I fall to the ground with him on top of me.

"Warn a guy next time," I groan, rubbing my ass that hit the hardwood.

"Sorry. But did you see that? I was amazing!" The excitement in Wes's voice makes the slight pain worth it.

"Is this what I can expect when you start hitting the

platform again? Nailing every dive and coming to tell me it was amazing?"

"If I didn't know how to dive, then yes. But I have no idea what I'm doing here. You're a very good teacher." Wes peppers my lips with kisses. The playfulness in him is palpable.

"Well, maybe if you beat me, I'll make it worth your while."

"Oh yeah?" Wes makes no move to get off of me. We're lying behind the ball return, our legs tangled together.

"I'll let you do that thing you really like doing." I waggle my eyebrows at him.

"How is that making it worth my while?" But I know he doesn't mean it, because I can feel him harden on top of me.

"Are you really telling me you don't want my ass when I can feel how much you want me?"

"This is so not the place for this conversation," Wes laughs.

"It's not. So let's get moving and we'll see who comes out on top."

Wes drops a lingering kiss. One full of promise for dirty things to come.

"Hmm, I do hope it's me."

Chapter Twenty-One

WES

"Have you ever done this before?" I sip the beer that Finn poured me from the foaming pitcher. It's rare that I have a drink, but I agreed to one with Finn.

"I haven't. I thought maybe we could try something that neither of us has done. Assuming you haven't done it…" Finn trails off.

"Nope. We're on even ground. We'll have to see who's better. Even though I still think it's unfair how badly you beat me at bowling."

"What can I say?" Finn drags a hand down my back, cupping my ass and pulling me into him. "I like being better than you at something, Mr. Athlete."

I don't know how we started this competition between the two of us. First bowling, now axe throwing. Instead of being turned on, every competitive bone in my body lights up.

"Oh, it's on, Finn. Prepare to go down."

"I'd say I am, but based on that gleam in your eye, we have very different meanings of that phrase right now."

"Tell you what." I line my feet up in the box, prepared to throw my axe. "If you win, I go down on you."

"And if you win?" Finn quirks a brow at me.

"And if I win, you go down on me." I chuck the blade like the worker showed us how to when we arrived, except it gets no purchase. It falls limply to the ground.

"Looks like someone will be going down on me then."

Finn hip checks me out of the way, sticking his tongue out, concentrating too hard at a game.

Right before he pulls back to throw, I go in for the kill. "Just think how good I'll look down on my knees for you."

The axe falls with a thud to the ground. "That is not fair." Finn turns a pointed finger on me.

"I have no idea what you're talking about." I take another sip of beer, ignoring the irate Finn as he goes to throw another axe. He mumbles something about cheating before taking another throw. It's hard not to love the way he's concentrating.

"Ha. Nailed it." A triumphant grin stretches across his face. Fuck, I'd lose just to see that smile on his face all the time. The more time I spend with him, the more my feelings grow. I never thought it would happen with Finn when he started his assignment. But now, it's one of the few things to pull my focus from diving.

"Hey, aren't you the Olympic diver?" A voice interrupts us from behind. I plaster on a smile, turning to find two women standing behind our booth. "Oh my gosh! It is you!"

"Hi, ladies. Are you having a nice night?" It still blows my mind that people recognize me for a sport that gains an international following for two weeks every four years.

"I told you it was him, Cassie. I recognize him from the articles being written about him."

"I'm always happy to meet fans."

"We'd love a picture, if you wouldn't mind. Then we promise we won't bother you anymore." She's clasping her hands, awaiting my answer.

"Sure thing." She shrieks and comes to stand next to me, letting her friend take the picture.

"You made my night, thank you so much! I hope you come back better than ever." And with that she's gone.

Taking the wind out of my sails with her.

"Does that happen a lot?" Finn questions as I sit on the stool next to him.

"They recognized me from the articles you're writing."

A blush creeps over his handsome face. "I'm sorry."

"Hey." I clasp a hand over his that's resting on the table. "I really should be thanking you."

"Why is that?" He sips on his beer, a foam mustache resting above his lip.

"Because I get recognized for a few weeks every couple of years then go back to relative anonymity. But maybe by bringing more attention to the sport, it'll make it more accessible to people."

"I guess I never thought of it like that."

Fisting Finn's shirt in my hand, I tug him close. "Don't think you're getting out of this bet we made because I'm distracted." I drop a lasting kiss on his lips, tasting the beer he's been drinking. A quiet moan escapes his lips, and I sink further into the kiss. It's better than any alcohol-induced haze. The sweet taste of Finn. The softness of his tongue as it tangles with mine. But just as quickly as it comes, it's gone.

"What were we talking about?" My brain is fuzzy after that kiss. Finn is the only thing in focus in the building.

"Wow, if you're that easy to distract, I'm going to be enjoying myself tonight."

"FUCK, WES." We don't make it past the front door before I'm pulling at Finn's belt, desperate to have his cock in my mouth. Finn upped the ante tonight, and I lost. In rather spectacular fashion. But I don't care. Because right now, Finn's cock is hanging out of his jeans, begging to be sucked, the turgid head leaking with excitement.

I don't spend another second staring before I take Finn to the back of my throat. "Shit." Finn arches into my mouth, his hands diving into my hair. His eyes are closed as his face twists in pleasure.

I pull off him. "Eyes open. I want to see you when you come down my throat."

The noises coming from him are unintelligible as I suck him in again, hollowing my cheeks to take as much of his hard length in my mouth as I can.

His blue eyes lock with mine. I've always liked a fast fuck. Get in, get off, get out. No connection. No feelings. Just pleasure. But not with Finn. He's cracked something open in me. I want to see every ounce of pleasure on his face as I bring him to release.

"Touch yourself." Finn's hands are in my hair, guiding me up and down his cock.

I smile around him, reaching into my pants and wrapping my hand around my own hard-as-steel cock. "Yes, just like that. I like knowing that sucking me off gets you off."

Fuck. If he's not careful, I'm going to come before him. I swipe my hand over the leaking head, using it to get myself closer to release.

"God, Wes. I'm getting close."

I reach my free hand around to play with his balls. I love knowing what brings pleasure to my man. It has my hand working faster. A few more long slides of my tongue under his cock and he's exploding down my throat. I suck every drop he gives me as I spill into my own hand. When I pull off him, he sinks to the floor. Glassy eyes meet mine. A dazed look on his face tells me he's sated.

"How's the winner of the evening feeling?" My voice is breathless. We're still clothed, not having made it far into my house. Sweat clings to Finn's shirt as he reaches for my hand, licking my own release off my hand.

"The winner is feeling quite good." Finn wraps an arm around me, tugging me into his side. We stay like this, wrapped up in each other in my entryway, legs tangled together, pants halfway down our thighs.

It's messy and raw, but I wouldn't change it for a thing. It's never been like this with anyone before. I always felt like I had to be on. And I'm scared for what it means. Because Finn and I can't work. He's writing about my return to diving, and the life of an Olympic athlete is anything but stable. I travel for a living and am gone too many months of the year. But being with Finn makes me want more.

I just don't know what more looks like for the two of us.

Chapter Twenty-Two

WES

Wiping the sweat from my brow, I throw my towel to the side and grab a drink of water. I've been pushing myself hard this week, but I feel good.

"You're looking good, kid. Think you're ready?" Damien comes up to stand beside me, his arms crossed in front of his chest.

"You know I am," I huff out.

"I'm putting together an exhibition of sorts. I want to bring some people in—some of your sponsors—and show that you're back."

"Don't you think that's a bit over the top?" I quirk a brow at him, resting a tired arm on the weight bar in front of me.

"No more than we're doing with Finn. Of course, he'll still have all access, but I want to put the world on notice that Wes Cooper is back and ready. Everyone will be champing at the bit to see you dive. I know I am."

"If you think that's the best way, then let's do it."

"Awesome. I'll set it up." Damien claps me on the shoulder and heads back to his office.

The shutting of the door in the quiet gym echoes around in my head. An exhibition for everyone to see me return to diving after being out the last few months.

Easy.

Something I could do in my sleep.

But dread like a lead weight settles in the pit of my stomach. I've been on the springboards and the five-meter platform. Taking that next step up to ten has been hanging over me like a black cloud.

I have dived off the ten-meter platform thousands of times. It's second nature to me. I should be able to do it in my sleep.

The air squeezes from my lungs as I think about it. Peering out the gym windows, the platforms are looming. They've always been there, steady. The one constant in my life in an otherwise chaotic existence. Diving has brought me comfort on my hardest days, when I didn't think I had anything left to give.

But these last few months have been more than hard. I've spent more sleepless nights stewing over my future than ever before. All because one man asked the hard question. As much as I care about Finn, it's still hard to show him this side of me. The one that is so uncertain about where I'll be in a few years.

Even if I haven't said it, I know a lot more is riding on my shoulders with these games next summer. Because what if I don't win? Will it mean everything I've accomplished is meaningless without that elusive Olympic victory?

I've never been scared of the platform, so why now?

"Doing okay?" Finn's voice jolts me out of my spiral of doom.

"Just talking with Damien about future events."

"The exhibition?" Finn rests his hip against the wall, turning to face me.

"He told you?"

"He wanted to make sure I knew I was the only one allowed behind the scenes. Everyone else would have to be out on the pool deck." Finn's confident smile tells me he likes being told where his place is.

"Do you think I'm ready?" I blurt out, in a very Finn-like manner.

"Really? You're asking me?" Finn moves a hand onto my forearm, pinning me with a serious look.

"Yes. You've been at my side almost every day since I came back to train. What do you think?"

Finn shakes his head. "I'm not who you need to be asking."

"But you're who I trust."

A warm look washes over Finn's face. "You are the most dedicated person I've ever met. Look around you. Everyone else has left, and you're still here, pushing. Fighting to gain every competitive inch you can."

I stare at my feet as if they are the most interesting things in the world. "You make me sound obsessive."

"Wes." Finn's fingers find my chin, bringing my gaze back to his. His eyes are calming behind his glasses. "I wish I had what it took to do what you do. But I don't. There is no one better suited to doing what you do than you. You inspire me."

"Really?" I push the words out, my mouth dry like sandpaper.

He nods his head. "Yes. Even though what we do is worlds apart, the dedication and drive you have for your work pushes me to be better."

"You kind of have a way with words, you know." Hooking a finger into the buttons on his shirt, I pull him closer, needing to breathe his air.

"I have a pretty good muse."

Dropping my forehead to his, I suck in a breath, my thoughts quieting. "Thank you, Finn. For believing in me."

Finn presses a soft, quick kiss to my lips. His whispered words fill every crack of my inside. "I'm here for you. I'm not going anywhere. And on the days where you don't quite believe in yourself, I'll have enough belief for both of us."

Chapter Twenty-Three

WES

Knocking on the door, I feel like I'm in high school again, picking up my boyfriend. I hadn't really thought through my idea of picking Finn up from his sister's when we planned tonight.

"Wes! Did you come to bake with me again?" A high-pitched voice rings up at me as the door swings open.

"Sorry, Darcy. Your Uncle Finn and I are going out tonight." Big blue eyes stare up at me, almost quizzically, like she can't make out what I would be doing here and not hanging out with her.

"Darcy. What did your mom tell you about opening the door to strangers?" Finn runs up behind her, his cheeks flaming red.

"I know him. So he's not a stranger." She turns back to face me. "He's been excited about your date all day."

"And that's enough from you. Go bug your mom." Finn spins her to send her on her way. "I think you missed the part where I said back door."

I wince. "Sorry. Will your sister be overbearing about this?"

"Will? That implies she hasn't been already. You'd think she was the reporter in the family, not me, the way she asks the questions." Finn steps outside, looking sexy as fuck in skinny jeans and a navy sweater. The way his dark hair is brushed back highlights his stunning features.

I laugh. "Is she always like that?"

"She's my big sister. Of course she is. She even drilled me about what time I'll be home."

I wince, hating that I can't tell Finn the real reason why I don't want him spending the night. It's a block I can't get past, no matter how much I wish I could.

"Sorry." It's hardly sufficient, but Finn doesn't notice.

"Now,"—Finn stuffs his hands in his pockets, leaning against my car— "what'd you find for us tonight?"

I lean closer, inhaling the pine scent that is all Finn, immediately feeling a calm wash over me. "Want to go to Paris?"

"We can't go to Paris." Finn's mouth hangs open, not quite catching on to my plans.

Reaching around Finn, I open the door, brushing against him. "You'd like Paris. History, wine, interesting people." I find his eyes locked on mine. "Kissing. Lots and lots of kissing."

"Kissing you say?" Finn runs a hand up my chest, heating my skin under the thickness of my sweater. His face is a breath away from mine. I can almost taste the minty toothpaste on his lips.

"Yes. Might be my favorite part."

The image strikes me, unbidden. Finn and me in Paris together, holding hands as we walk along the Seine. Ignoring all the sights because the two of us are so in love, we're all we see.

Finn presses a kiss to my lips and gets in the car. He pulls me back to the present, to outside his sister's house.

The picture was so vibrant that it felt, even for that split second, I was with Finn in Paris.

I get back to telling him about our planned evening. "While I'd love to be kissing you in Paris, tonight will have to be a good close second. I found a painting studio where we can paint the Eiffel Tower, and as a bonus for you, it is something I've never tried before."

I move around the car, getting in and taking Finn's hand in mine. "You've really never painted before?" he asks.

Squeezing his hand, I point the car in the direction of the small studio I found. "I promise. Although, it probably would've been a good hobby to take up during recovery."

"Why's that?"

"Something to take my mind off the fact that diving was no longer my sole focus in life."

"Bit of an existential crisis?" Finn asks, turning to face me.

"I guess you could say that. I was faced with my own mortality, of sorts."

Finn drops my hand, crossing his arms and leaning against the car door. "That's quite doom and gloom. Even for you."

"I'm serious." Pulling up to a stoplight, I face him full-on. "I think it's a moment every athlete has. The possibility that the end is much closer than they feared."

"And is your end closer?" Finn, ever the reporter, always knows the question to ask that hits me in a way I'm not prepared for.

"I think it is, yes. At least, I'm closer to the end now than I am the beginning. My body isn't what it used to be."

A honk causes me to jolt and proceed through the green light.

"Yes, because I imagine your body before was terrible. All lumps and bumps and not magazine worthy."

A blush creeps up my neck, one that only seems to come out when Finn is around. "I'm serious. I have to get steroid shots to help with joint pain. I tape my hands to help absorb the shock of going into the water at thirty-five miles an hour. If I have a bad day of training, I feel it for a week."

"I'm in awe of you, you know." Chancing a glance at Finn, his eyes are locked on me, unwavering.

"Why? I'm not changing the world." It's a callous tone I take, but Finn calls me out on it.

"Sure, you're not at the edge of critical research that will cure a life-threatening disease, but you matter. You're someone who is persevering after an injury, and to many that's inspiring. You don't have to change the world to change someone's life."

"You have quite a way with words, you know that?" Finn's words hit deep. Winning or losing, that's been my focus. There was never time to reevaluate anything because training was always on my mind. Even if I can't fully process his words, they'll stay with me. Because the man sitting next to me is slowly embedding himself into the fabric of my being.

"It's a good thing it's my life's passion then."

"Are you ready to make this your life's passion?" I pull into the parking lot of the art studio. Paintings hang in the windows, neon lights flashing that anyone is welcome.

"Care to make a wager?"

"What is it with you and betting?" I take his hand in mine, walking into the bright studio. I never used to be one for physical touch, but with Finn, I crave it. It's like my body knows I need to be near him to be calm. Settled.

"Last time it didn't work out so well."

I tap on the screen, checking us in. Leaning in close, I nip at his ear. "Is this you trying to leverage a blow job? Because I'll happily go down on you right here."

Finn discreetly adjusts himself as an older woman comes over to guide us to our easels for the night. "We'll begin shortly, gentlemen. I hope you're ready to paint the Eiffel Tower in all her glory tonight."

"Thank you," I say to her retreating back as she helps the next guests. "Now, back to this bet. What did you have in mind?"

"Based on that conniving look on your face, I think you have something in mind." A finger circles in front of my face.

"I do. And it's not what you think, Mr. Anderson."

Understanding washes over Finn's face. "Oh no. No way. I am not doing another day of training with you."

Laughter bursts out of me. "Well then, I guess you're going to have to paint better than I do."

Finn grabs me, pulling me in close. The sparkle in his blue eyes is electric. "You're on. And I know what I want if I win."

"A blow job?" I whisper against his pillow soft lips.

"No. Bragging rights that I beat you."

"Then." Kiss. "Bragging rights." Kiss. "It shall be." Kiss.

I go to pull back but Finn's hand finds the back of my head, locking me to him. His tongue traces the seam of my lips, teasing, tasting, but not entering. It's the tiniest bit of foreplay, making me drunk with need.

"Good evening, everyone. I hope you're ready for an evening in Paris, because we are about to be whisked away." The instructor calls our attention to her.

"Saved by the teacher, it seems." I fight the glare breaking through at the tease next to me.

"Best get ready, Cooper, because I plan on winning."

"You're on."

My competitive nature comes out in full force, paying attention to each stroke and brush move she makes on the canvas. Finn's tongue pokes out between his lips, his concentration on the canvas in front of him.

The soft sounds of the studio fade to the background as I put the finishing touches on my masterpiece as the class winds down.

"Alright, everyone. If you haven't already completed your painting, we'll be coming around to offer any assistance. We hope you've enjoyed this evening."

Setting my brush in the murky water, I peruse the final product in front of me.

"What in the world is that?" Finn snorts next to me, eyeing my painting.

"The Eiffel Tower." I steal a glance at his. "What in the world is *that*?"

"The Eiffel Tower." We parrot each other's words back to one another. "I followed every step without fail."

I lean closer, examining the shape. When it finally hits me, a deep, belly laugh escapes.

"What? Why are you laughing like that?" Finn looks between me and his canvas.

"It looks like a hairy cock and balls."

His jaw drops in shock. "It does not!"

"Oh my God. It so does! I should be worried if this is what you think of mine."

"You'll be lucky if I go near yours now." Finn rolls his eyes, the smirk on his lips betraying his amusement. "Besides, yours doesn't look anything like the real thing."

"Better than a cock and balls."

"It looks like a rocket ship." He points out the shape on my canvas with his brush, the tip glancing over one spot.

"Hey, no destroying my painting. This will be framed in the Louvre one day."

"Oh yeah?" Eyes locked with mine, Finn drags his wet paint brush through the swirling colors on my canvas.

"You little shit." Dragging my finger through my own paint, I shove him back and reach across, running a finger through his canvas.

"You ruined my masterpiece!"

"You ruined mine first!" I echo. Swiping my wet finger across his cheek, I mark it with the pink paint now smudged on his canvas. Smugness is thick in the air as we each stare at one another.

Before I know what happens, Finn dips a finger in his remaining paint and splashes it across my face. "I'll just create another one then."

"So you're calling me a masterpiece, huh?"

"With my help, you will be." Finn's fingers move through the cool, sticky substance on my face.

"Then let me make you one yourself." I grab his face, pulling him to me, rubbing my face all over his.

"Uhh, excuse me. But we ask that you not paint each other." The instructor is standing in front of our easels, glancing between the two of us like we're toddlers. No doubt Finn's face matches my own, blue and pink paint coating his handsome features.

"Right. Sorry about that," Finn apologizes. Even I can see the pink hue creeping up his cheeks under the blue dye.

"Who knew you were such a bad influence?" I chuckle, pulling Finn in for a kiss. The smell of paint is pungent this close to him.

"What can I say? I didn't want you winning."

"I think you lose by default."

"You never said we couldn't play dirty," he quips.

"Then I guess we'll have to come back. Be that couple who paints together."

Finn bellows out a laugh. "God, I hope not. They'll never let us back."

Chapter Twenty-Four

WES

"Are we allowed to be in here?" Finn can't hide the nervousness from his voice.

"Relax. It's fine." I pull the door shut behind me, pushing Finn farther into the aquatic center. "Damien gave me a key. He wouldn't do that if he didn't trust me."

"Still, this feels…nefarious."

I snort out a laugh. "Nefarious? Are you some evil genius in your spare time?" I spin Finn around, backing him up against the wall.

"You haven't caught on? I'm an evil genius who has set out to lure you under my spell." Finn's lips curl up into a smile. I'd laugh if the statement wasn't true.

"Then I must say you've succeeded." I drop a quick kiss on his lips, smiling as he follows my retreating mouth. "C'mon."

Linking my fingers with his, I drag him out onto the pool deck. With all the lights off, save a few for security bulbs, it's dark.

"Why'd you want to bring me here?" Finn's voice

echoes around the cavernous building. With no one in here, it's even louder than normal.

"I wanted you to experience this how I see it."

"In the dark with no people?"

"Are you always this cheeky?" Wrapping an arm around Finn's shoulders, I bring him closer to me.

"What can I say? I guess you just bring it out in me." A lingering hand moves around my waist, pulling me to him. "Besides, someone has to keep you in check."

"I like that it's you." Sincerity is etched in my tone. A loving look washes over Finn's face.

"And I like that you bring out this side in me."

"Your nefarious side?"

Finn shoves me but doesn't go far. I'm still wrapped in his embrace. Exactly where I want to be.

"No. This adventurous side. You make me feel like I can do anything and it's possible. Like I can grab life by the balls and it'll turn out okay."

I lean closer, my lips a breath away from his. "As long as you're not grabbing anyone else's balls, it'll be okay."

I steal a kiss before Finn can protest.

"So why are we here?" Finn's voice is breathless. It stirs something inside me that I bring out this reaction in him.

I sigh, spinning around to take in my surroundings. "I feel like I've been going a thousand miles a minute since I came back and just haven't taken a minute to myself. It kind of feels overwhelming."

"Are you nervous about the exhibition?"

Walking around the deck, my gaze finds the diving platforms. "I've been diving for thirteen years. It's second nature."

"That doesn't answer my question." Finn's fists are pinned on his hips, staring at me from across the pool now.

"I'll be ready." I take a breath, adding more force to my voice. "I am ready."

I don't know who I say it more for—him or me. But the closer next week's exhibition gets, the more the pressure has been weighing on me. With each passing day, I can feel the excitement building within the club. Everyone is ready for me to get back on the platform. Everyone but me, that is.

"Would it help if you did some dives now? Just for me?" Finn nudges my shoulder with his.

I turn, finding his handsome face only inches from mine. "Want to do something else to make me feel better?"

"Okay, now I know you have something nefarious in mind."

I don't miss the heat in his eyes, the lust dripping from his words.

"Why would you ever think that?" Finding the hem of his shirt, my hands drift up his stomach, catching his hard nipples. A groan rips from his throat as I pull his shirt over his head and toss it at our feet.

"You are a bad influence," Finn whispers before giving me a searing kiss. His tongue demands entry and I grant it, letting him control this kiss. My hands find his hair, fisting it to keep him exactly where he is. The desire and need is palpable as my tongue tangles with his.

"Get naked," I command. Finn's lips are working their way down my jaw, nipping and sucking as they go. I'm hard as a rock.

"Here?" Finn pulls back, his glasses askew.

"Yes." Grabbing him by the belt, I undo it and shove his pants, boxer briefs and all, down to his ankles. His hard cock pops out, smacking him in the stomach. "You're not following instructions very well."

Finn is standing before me as I start to disrobe. He

kicks into gear just as I drop my pants. Kicking off his shoes, I grab his hand and walk backward toward the pool. "Ever been skinny-dipping?"

"What?"

Before he has time to overthink, I wrap my arms around him and dive us both into the pool. Finn comes up sputtering, wiping the water from his eyes. "A little more warning would be nice next time."

"So you want to make this a thing?" I swim toward him as he sets his glasses on the edge of the pool. Caging him in, the heat rolling off his body is evident.

"Being naked with you? Yes." His hands come up, cupping my face. "I very much want to make this a thing. An everyday thing, in fact."

My hands find his hips, anchoring him to me. His hard cock brushes along my own equally hard one. Water clings to Finn's eyelashes, his blue eyes dark with need and desire, no doubt mirroring my own.

But there's more than just need and desire swirling in his eyes. It's the love there that has me blurting out my next words. "I love you."

"You what?" Shock now colors Finn's face and has me pulling back from him. I don't think I misread his feelings for me.

"I know it's soon. And I have the most chaotic life and I'm still technically the subject you're writing about, but I can't help it. I've gone and fallen stupidly in love with you and—"

Finn's fingers on my lips cut off my rambling. I send up a silent prayer of thanks before his mouth replaces his fingers. It's sweet, tender, and has my entire body vibrating with need for the man doing it.

"Is that what I sound like when I start rambling?" Finn drops his forehead to mine, his fingers caressing my lips.

"More or less," I say on a laugh.

"Well, I'm glad you love me then and will put up with it, because it probably won't stop anytime soon. It makes me love you just a bit more that I can turn you into a rambling fool."

"You love me?" My hand drops to Finn's chest, tracing the small pattern of freckles there.

He nods his head. "Yes. I love you, Wes. I never expected to fall in love while on this assignment, but I did. I love being with you. It's fun and easy and better than I ever imagined. And that's all I want."

I capture his lips with mine. Standing here, shoulder-deep in the shallow end of the pool, I know this is a moment that will be burned into my memory for a lifetime. I've never felt this way before. It's like this one kiss is wiping away every kiss before it. All I know, all I'll ever want to know, is the softness of Finn's lips. The way they know mine. How they can drive me into a fury of need and want and lust in a matter of seconds.

My wandering hand finds our hard cocks. Taking both in my hand, I give a hard stroke.

"Mmm. Harder." Finn mumbles against my lips. His hand reaches down, enclosing around mine.

"Like that?" I give us a hard squeeze, relishing the way his cock feels against my own.

"Yes." Finn's free hand clasps the back of my neck. "So good."

I drag my hand up, slowly stroking us. Finn's head drops back, moans of delight escaping his lips. The vein in his neck is pulsing, aching to be kissed. I take my time with him, working him over while my lips nip and suck at his neck, licking over his Adam's apple.

"Wes." Finn's hand squeezes harder over mine, telling me what he needs.

"I know." Wrapping one of Finn's legs around my hips, my other hand dips lower, playing with his balls.

"Shit. I'm going to come." Locking eyes with Finn, I don't stop stroking him until he's shouting out his release. His flushed skin, hazy eyes, and loose body pulls my own orgasm from me, both of us coming together in a rush.

Our breaths are the only thing I hear, echoing in the small space around us.

"Shit, Finn. That was…"

"Out of this world," he finishes.

I drop my head to his chest, the rapid beat of his heart doing nothing to calm my own.

"Yeah." I drop a kiss to his chest as a loud bang has me perking up.

"Who's there?" A voice bellows from the far reaches of the pool deck.

"Shit." A flashlight points directly toward us.

"Pool's closed." I recognize the voice as it comes closer.

"Dive down a bit. I'll get him out of here," I whisper against Finn's lips.

"Who is it?" He sinks down, his head floating just below the lip of the pool.

"Roger. Security guard."

"Hey, Roger. It's just me." I give a wave, not daring to move from the wall, lest I show him exactly what is going on here.

"Oh, Wes. Sorry. Didn't realize it was you."

"Just came for some extra practice." I thumb over my shoulder, pointing to the platforms behind me. Like he wouldn't know what I was doing.

"You almost finished?"

"Yeah. I'll lock up when I'm done."

Roger nods his head, turning and walking back to where he came from. Once he's out of sight, I look down at Finn. The look of distress on his face has me barking out in laughter.

"How are you laughing? What if we were caught?" Finn's eyes are crazed as he looks around us. "I could've been fired!"

"I think you're being a bit dramatic. No one is firing anyone."

"Easy for you to say. You're the king of the pool."

"Oh yeah?" I drop an arm behind Finn on the deck, sinking in closer to him.

"Yes. Now we need to go before we get caught again." Finn lifts himself out of the pool, water sliding down his lithe body. A pained moan escapes my lips. What I wouldn't give to still have him here in front of me, right where I want him most.

"Isn't that part of the fun? Almost getting caught?" I get out of the pool, dripping wet, by our clothes as Finn furiously puts his on.

"I knew you had a nefarious plan."

I grab Finn by his wrist, halting his movements. "This?" I waggle a finger between us and the pool. "That was not my plan. There was nothing nefarious about it. What I plan to do to you later?" I step closer, allowing Finn to feel my hardening dick. He audibly gulps. "That will be nefarious."

Chapter Twenty-Five

WES

"You're looking good, Wes. Tomorrow is going to be a good day."

I nod at Damien, trying to ignore the nerves that have been licking at the edges of my consciousness all day. The shift from being here last night with Finn compared to now is potent.

I was calm being wrapped up in Finn's arms. But now, it's the nerves that are taking center stage. The ten-meter platform is looming large over me. It's been too long since I've been up there. Damien wanted my first time back up there to be big.

But the pressure has been building and it's too much. Looking around the pool, I find Finn talking with Simone. Even the sight of him doesn't do much to calm me.

"I'm just ready to put it behind me and focus on the qualifiers. That's what I should be focusing on."

"Yeah, but this will show the world that you're back and you're the one to beat," Damien says, clapping me on the shoulder.

"I'm going to go ice down and then head home for the

day if that's alright." I thumb behind me, not looking for approval as I head back toward the locker room. Waving at the trainer, they draw up an ice bath for me as I sink in, waiting for the cold to take over.

This is everything I've been working for, so why is the anxiety building now? I thrive under pressure. What was it that I told Finn? That I can block everything out when I'm up there and just focus on the dive.

But now it's different. The only thing I can focus on is what might go wrong. What if I step the wrong way and reinjure myself and lose myself in the air? It's something that could happen on any dive to any diver. Instead of focusing on my dives for tomorrow, I just keep thinking about the worst-case scenario happening.

Why, instead of visualizing myself executing the perfect dive, am I seeing myself crashing into the water at an odd angle and hurting myself worse than before? Ice—colder than the bath I'm sitting in—settles in my gut. I don't know if I can admit that I can't do it. That maybe I need more time.

"You done for the day?" Finn's voice startles me out of my spiral.

"Shit, you scared me."

"I called your name. Are you okay?" Running a hand through my hair, I lean into his warmth.

"Sorry. Just in my head about tomorrow."

"We can take it easy tonight. I won't stay long."

I push out of the tub, not knowing how long I've been in here. "You can stay. It's okay."

"Are you sure?" Finn questions.

I nod. Maybe having him around tonight will help calm me down.

"And then tomorrow we'll celebrate a great exhibition."

The pride in Finn's eyes is crushing. I know it's a big moment for me, but he's been with me every step of the way through this too. And he's excited for me.

So how can I look him in the eyes and *not* do this tomorrow?

I've done this my entire life. So I can push down whatever this is that I'm feeling and do this for Finn.

Finn

"HOW ARE YOU FEELING ABOUT TOMORROW?" I gaze down into Wes's brown eyes. We've been binging the latest Netflix series this past week. The closer the exhibition has gotten, the more tension I can see building in him. He doesn't do a good job hiding it.

"It'll be good to get back out there," Wes sighs.

"You know it's okay to be nervous."

Wes sits up, resting his back against the side of the couch. "What makes you think I'm nervous?"

The defensiveness in his tone makes me sit up straighter and take notice. "It's the first time you're getting back on the ten-meter. Even I know that's a big deal."

"Well it's not." He turns, facing the TV, ending the conversation. His shoulders are up by his ears.

"I'm going to go make dinner." I stand, dropping a kiss on his head. He doesn't acknowledge me. His tension permeates the air, and I'm like a sponge soaking it up.

I'm not used to this Wes. I'm used to the confident, strong guy who takes command of any room he is in. The one sitting in the living room, staring off into space, is ignoring me the best he can.

Ever since Wes's coach announced that they were making a big event of Wes returning to diving, I was excited. I haven't seen him dive from that high platform yet. Sure, I've watched videos from before his injury, but it's not something I've seen in person.

Wes is a specimen when he dives. The way he moves and contorts his body as he slings himself into the air and into the water is an art form.

But now a prickly feeling is poking at the edges as I start dinner. Even with everything that Wes has had going on these last few weeks, he's still been supportive of my writing. It felt weird writing about him once we started our relationship, but it didn't faze him.

There's something that's bothering him now, and I wish he would lean on me. I can't imagine the pressure that Wes is under as an elite athlete. Even I can spot the difference between those who are competing for a medal and those that are training for a chance to even make it to the Olympics.

Wes is the star of the club. Everyone gives him respect. He's earned it. But now I'm worried about at what cost.

"Need some help?" Wes's arms around me cause me to jump out of my skin.

"Shit. Don't sneak up on me like that."

Wes kisses my shoulder. "Sorry. Wanted to see if I could help." He gives me a shy smile. Some of the earlier tension has eased.

"Want to get the salad started?"

"Sure thing." He squeezes my side and starts working next to me. "I'm doing okay, you know."

Turning, I find an easy smile on Wes's face. It's a facade. His eyes give him away. They aren't the deep brown I'm used to seeing shine.

"It will be exciting to see you dive tomorrow."

"You've seen me dive," he quips.

I roll my eyes. "I know, but not from ten meters. It's exciting."

Wes sets the salad bowl aside, taking my hand in his. "It'll be easier knowing you're out there watching tomorrow."

"It doesn't make you more nervous that I'll be there?"

He shakes his head. "No. It'll be calming, actually. Almost like I'll be performing just for you."

I start to walk backward, pulling Wes with me. "I've got another way that might help calm you down for tomorrow."

"I already like where this is going." The smile on Wes's face is brighter than it has been all day.

"Don't get that excited." I tug Wes into his bedroom, pushing him down on his stomach. "I think a back rub might help."

"You're such a tease." Wes's voice is muffled against the pillows as I dig my hands into his back. "Oh shit."

"Sorry, what was that?" It's hard not to keep the knowing tone from my voice.

"Do that again. That feels amazing."

"So bossy," I laugh.

"Hey, you're the one that brought me in here." The knots in Wes's back tell me more than he's been letting on. I know this is what he does for a living, but he's carrying the weight of all the expectations, quite literally, on his shoulders.

All I hear are Wes's grunts as I continue kneading the muscles in his back. I don't know the first thing about performing on the world stage, but if I can do this, even help ease the tension in one small way, I'll do it. I'll do anything for Wes.

Somewhere along the way, Wes became so much more

than a means to get ahead in my career. Sure, he's inspiring me in ways I never thought I would be, but the love I feel for this man? I never thought I'd know something like this. The passion Wes shows for diving is nothing compared to the passion I feel when he looks at me.

And it scares me. Because Wes's life is unpredictable. He travels, has events, and is pulled in so many different directions, I can't even begin to keep track.

But I want to. I want to have a part in his life. Because this thing between us isn't ending when my assignment does.

And that's the scariest part. Making this work when we're from two different worlds.

"MORNING," I say to Wes, who is standing in the kitchen, his breakfast sitting in front of him. His face is pale, ashen.

"Hey." His soft, sleep-filled voice isn't comforting. After last night, I thought Wes would be doing better this morning. But he looks more off than I've ever seen him.

"Today's the day." There's not much else I can say. I'm worried anything else might set him off.

Wes nods, gulping down the rest of his coffee. "I'm getting ready to head out. I'll see you after?"

"I'll be the one cheering the loudest for you." That pulls a smirk from his handsome face.

"I think you might be losing your journalistic credibility."

"I'll have you know I'm still unbiased when it comes to you." Wes quirks a brow in my direction as I move to wrap my arms around him. "Not one single article has talked about what a cute ass you have."

"Oh, my mistake then."

Wes's hands ball into fists on my chest, his eyes locked on them. "Is it bad that I'm ready for this to be over?"

I cup his jaw, tilting his face up to meet mine. "Just do what you've always done. You've got this."

I bring my lips to his, letting him know I'm here with him. His hands tighten in my shirt, clutching me to him. "Thank you, Finn. I don't know if I could do this without you there today."

Dropping my forehead to his, I tell him the truth. "You could have, but you won't have to." I take a deep breath. "I love you, Wes. No matter where we end up, I'll always love you and support you. In anything you do."

Wes kisses me, a soul-stirring, life-affirming kiss. Like he might float away if I am not here anchoring him to the world. "I love you, Finn. Thank you for being here for me. I don't think I have the right words to tell you what it means to me."

Hugging Wes to me, we stand in the kitchen for who knows how long. "I know. Now go out there and do what you do best."

Chapter Twenty-Six

WES

The aquatic center dominates the skyline in front of me. I've been sitting in my car for the last twenty minutes, trying to get out.

Today's the day.

Finn's words ring through my head. I'll either sink or swim, quite literally, at the end of the event. Taking a deep breath, I open my door and head into the center.

I ignore the shouts and cheers as I walk back into the locker room.

I ignore Damien and his tips as I warm up my body.

Ignore.

Ignore.

Ignore.

It's all I can do to keep putting one foot in front of the other when everyone starts heading out to the pool deck.

"Ready, Wes?" Damien slaps me on the shoulder. The grin on his face tells me how proud he is of me.

"As I'll ever be." Thank God I'm only training for individual events. I don't know what I'd do if it was synchro. Walking out onto the deck, the faces all blur together. I try to pick out Finn, a lighthouse in the storm in my head, but it's too hard.

"You're last up of the five. You've done this before, so you've got nothing to worry about." Damien's words try to be encouraging, but all they do is irritate me.

Why the fuck do people keep saying I've done this before? I've never come back from an injury like this. I've been dreading this. Every time I picture myself diving, I see myself hitting the platform wrong and hurting myself before falling into the pool and hurting myself even worse.

I watch the divers before me, performing dives I've done my entire life. The tucks are making my head spin.

"You're on deck." I don't know who tells me this, but my feet start moving up the tower, passing the one-meter, three-meter and five-meter.

The smell of chlorine is strong, stinging my eyes. The pounding in my head increases as my feet hit the ten-meter. Two steps forward, and it's harder to breathe. The lights are brighter up here. Too bright.

I know I need to walk to the edge, but I'm stuck. My feet are in quicksand, unable to move. The lead weight is heavier now, pushing down on me so it's a struggle to breathe. My head is starting to get fuzzy, the aquatic center swirling in front of me.

Pain radiates through my knees. I'm not sure when I collapse, but I'm bent over on the platform, struggling to breathe.

Is this what a heart attack feels like?

Dropping my head to the cool concrete of the platform, I try to steady my breathing, but I can't. My heart feels like it's going to beat out of my chest.

"Wes."

"What are you doing here?" Finn's voice puzzles me. Confusion settles in as I try to figure out what's going on.

"C'mon." Strong arms wrap around me, pulling me off the ground. I don't think—I latch on, clinging onto Finn for dear life.

Voices reach my ears as the drone quiets around me. The buzzing in my head is softer now.

"Is he going to be okay?"

"The doctor will be in shortly."

"Can you sit?" Finn whispers in my ear.

I nod as he sets me down, but I don't let go. Finn is the only tether I have from losing it, even more than I already have. His hand is moving through my hair. I close my eyes, leaning into his touch.

"What's wrong, Wes?" A new voice enters the room.

People keep talking around me. The only thing I can focus on is Finn.

"Can I have a minute with him?" he asks. "Please?"

The closing of a door startles me.

"Wes. Talk to me." Fear is evident in his tone.

"It feels like I'm having a heart attack." I try to take deep breaths, but it's hard. An anvil is pushing down on my chest, and I can't breathe.

"You're not. Deep breaths." He moves my hand over his heart, the steady thumping easy to track.

"Take me home?" I hate how small my voice sounds.

Finn doesn't hesitate, helping me pull on my sweats. My hands are shaking as the world starts spinning again. I reach out toward Finn, and he pulls me into his embrace.

"I'm here. I'm not going anywhere."

His words cause the floodgates to open. All the pain and emotion come pouring out. Sobs break out as Finn hugs me closer to him.

"It's okay, Wes. It's okay."

"Is it though?" My voice is muffled against his chest. I can barely begin to process what just happened.

Finn pulls back, wiping away the tears on my face. "Whatever happened out there today, it doesn't matter. What matters is that I'm here and you're not alone." His voice is firm, leaving no room for argument.

He takes my hand, pulling me up. Securing an arm around my shoulders, he leads me through the empty halls and out to his car. I close my eyes, trying to quell the tears still trailing down my face. Finn's hand squeezes my thigh.

The drive through the city to my house is short. Finn comes around and opens my door. Standing on shaky legs, I lean on him as he walks me inside. I've never felt so helpless.

"Time to rest."

I don't have room in me to argue with him. Stripping off my shirt, I fall into the softness of my sheets. Taking the first deep breath of the day, I find comfort in Finn.

"I'm here." Finn says those words again, curling himself around me. He's whispered them over and over today, but they're grounding me. The strength of his hold stills the thoughts racing through my head, enough to lure me into sleep.

I DON'T KNOW how much time passes before I wake up, the furthest thing from a restful sleep.

"Hi." Finn sweeps my hair out of my eyes. He looks about as bad as I feel.

Resting his hand on my cheek, his eyes never leave mine. The sun is setting outside the window.

"How badly did I fuck up?"

"You didn't fuck up." Finn pulls me into his chest. "God, Wes. When you collapsed up there, every terrible thought went through my head."

I wince. The last thing I want is to cause the man I love any pain. "I'm sorry."

"Don't be sorry. Talk to me. What happened up there?"

I scrub a hand down my face. "I don't know. All the pressure just kept building. I couldn't sleep and the only thing I could think about was Damien telling me how great it was going to be to get back up there. And because I didn't listen to him the first time, I figured I'd be fine doing it for the first time in front of everyone. But it wasn't and I cracked."

"Why didn't you tell me?" Concern crosses his face. "Is you not sleeping why you've never wanted me to spend the night here?"

Finn scoots down the bed, lying on his side to face me. I trace the muscle on his check. The shame takes hold as I nod. "I didn't want you to see me like this because I was embarrassed. I'm an elite athlete. I've won the World Cup, yet an exhibition just to see me dive pushes me off the deep end? No offense, Finn, but the press would chew me up and spit me back out."

"I wish you would've told me. This is different—your first event since an injury." Finn cups my cheek, his thumb tracing the hard line of my jaw. "It's okay to not be okay."

"Is it though? I'm expected to be able to handle the pressure and deal with it."

The caring look in Finn's eyes is almost more than I deserve. "You had a panic attack. No one expects you to deal with that."

"It felt like I was having a heart attack."

"It does feel like that. The number of times Melissa was at the ER when she was younger because she thought she was dying…" Finn trails off.

"Your sister had them?"

He nods. "She did. It took a lot of years for her to realize what they were and how to handle them. They aren't easy."

I thread my fingers through his hair. "I hate that you're so familiar with them."

"And yet I completely missed that you were about to break down."

I shake my head. "I don't know if I would've admitted it. I didn't want you to see it. If I had, it would've felt like I was letting everyone down. You, Damien, my mom, my teammates. I didn't want you to see my weakness."

"It's not a weakness to admit when you need more time or help."

"Yeah, but diving is who I am."

Finn takes me in his arms again, his heart beating a rapid pace beneath my ear. "No. Diving is what you do. It's not who you are."

And that triggers the scariest question today.

"And who am I without diving?"

Chapter Twenty-Seven

FINN

"Are you feeling any better this morning?"

Purple shadows mar the skin underneath Wes's eyes—tired brown eyes that don't hold their usual glow.

"I mean, not great, but better than yesterday." Wes lets out a heavy sigh. It's been a long few days since the exhibition. For not ever spending the night here, you couldn't peel me away from Wes's side now. Work has been breathing down my neck on what's going on between the two of us and if I'll be able to publish an article on Wes if I'm fucking him. My editor's words, not mine. Wes's coach has called daily to check on him, and I think it only adds to the pressure he's putting on himself.

"I can stay home with you today if you want." I brush a lock of hair out of his face.

"What do you have planned for today?"

"Harry wants to see me. The article is running today, so he wants me in the office. I can blow him off." For all the talk of wanting this assignment to push my career to the next level, right now, in this moment, I couldn't give a fuck. Wes and his well-being are more important right now.

But after Wes read the article, he wouldn't let me *not* publish it. He said it was too important and could help so many more people. So I wrote it. I poured everything I had into it. For Wes and for anyone else who was struggling.

"It's okay. I'll be fine until you get back." The sigh in his words guts me.

"Are you sure? I have Darcy's birthday party later tonight."

Wes drops his head back against the bed, looking over at me as I finish getting dressed. I haven't left his house since his panic attack.

"Finn. I'm not going to break. You can go to work and a birthday party without worrying about me."

"I know that. But it doesn't mean I'm not going to be concerned about the man I love."

Wes sits up, scooting on his knees over to me. Grabbing me by the tie, he pulls me close to him. "Why don't you go to the office and then we'll both go to Darcy's party tonight."

"It's a unicorn-themed pool party," I say, wrapping my arms around his waist.

"Well, if it wasn't a unicorn-themed party, I don't think I'd be able to go." The small smile that graces his lips is the first one I've seen in a week, and it settles something inside of me. That maybe, just maybe, he'll be okay.

"I know she'll be happy to see you. You'd think I'm chopped liver, because she only asks to see you."

Wes's hands wrap around my neck, bringing my lips down to his. "What can I say? I'm a cool person."

"Yeah, yeah." I pinch his side. "I'll be back as soon as I meet with Harry."

Wes's face drops. "How much trouble are you in?"

"With the article I wrote, hopefully not much. But that's not for you to worry about."

I kiss the quirk of Wes's lips. "How'd you know I'd be worrying?"

"Because I can see it in your eyes. The only thing you need to worry about right now is not stressing about anything."

"Does that actually work? Telling someone not to worry?"

I shrug my shoulders. "I can hope. Besides—" A knock at the front door cuts me off.

"You finish getting ready and I'll get the door." Wes steps off the bed, his gray sweats hanging low on his hips.

I don't waste time, wanting to know who's at the door. Muffled voices make their way back to me as I grab my jacket and head out into the living room.

Damien is sitting on the couch, relaxed as he can be.

"Finn. Good to see you." He nods his head at me as Wes sits across from him.

"What are you doing here?" I can't hide the defensiveness in my tone. It's been a hard few days. I don't want Damien here adding any more weight to Wes's already heavy shoulders.

Damien throws his hands up in defense. "Relax. I'm just here to check in on Wes."

"Go to work. We'll be fine." Wes nods at me. I've lost count of the number of times he's said he's fine now.

"Call me if you need me?" I ask, dropping a kiss on his lips, wishing I could stay here all day.

"I will. Love you."

"I love you."

WES

"NOW THAT YOUR keeper is gone, how are you feeling?" Damien asks when the door closes.

I fight the urge to smack Damien. "Finn has been nothing short of amazing the last few days. So if you're going to criticize him, then you can leave right now."

It wasn't Damien's fault or Finn's fault that I had a meltdown. But damn if I will let him sit here and criticize Finn. If it weren't for him, I don't know where I would be right now.

"Sorry. I really did want to see how you were doing."

Question of the hour.

I've been asking myself that ever since Finn brought me down from the platform. "Honestly, I don't know. Better than I was, but I just feel like I'm floating right now."

Damien rests his elbows on his knees, his brows pinched. "Did I put too much pressure on you? If I'd known you weren't doing well, I would've backed off."

My head shakes on its own accord. "No. I put it on myself. I had my doubts before the exhibition, and I didn't say anything."

"You're taking time off."

"Damien—"

He cuts me off. "No. There is no compelling argument you can give me right now that would convince me you're in the right mindset for training."

"I wasn't going to argue. I just want to know if I still have a spot with the team if I come back."

"If?" Damien's voice is panicked now.

Did I really mean *if?* The sick feeling that's been my

constant companion the last few days comes back with a vengeance.

"I want to say I'll come back for sure, but I can't make any promises right now."

Damien nods his head, standing and shoving his hands in his pockets. "I'll support you with whatever you decide to do. You'll always have a spot on the team, so when you're ready, call me, but not a day before."

I stand, reaching my hand out to Damien, but he knocks it away and pulls me in for a hug. "As a friend, take care of yourself. I don't want to see you hurting like this."

I smile, giving him an extra squeeze. "Thanks Damien. I appreciate it."

"And make sure Finn knows I didn't pressure you to come back. I don't want him coming after me."

A laugh burbles out of me, the first time in days. It feels awkward and good all at the same time. "He wouldn't have left if he actually thought you would try to push me back to the pool too soon."

"Someone like Finn is a keeper, and I mean that in a good way. Don't let him go."

I shake my head. "Not a chance in hell."

Mental Health and The Elite Athlete: When is it too much?
By Finn Anderson

We cheer them on and glorify their achievements. When they step onto their field of play, broken down and bloody, we launch them into a stratosphere of their own making. But what happens when they can't do it?

We vilify them. We ridicule them and tear them down. Why couldn't they play hurt? Why couldn't they suffer through broken bones and strained limbs and illness to win at the elite level they've trained their whole lives for?

These athletes push their bodies harder than any normal person would ever dream. If we're sick, we can lie in bed all day and recover. But when someone plays at the elite level, demands are made of them and their body.

If you've been following along on my series, you know that world-renowned diver Wes Cooper has had a grueling training schedule to even think about coming back to the diving world. After an unfortunate Achilles injury, I saw the blood, sweat, and tears he put into his rehab. The early mornings, even earlier nights. And all for the sake of throwing himself off a three-story platform that gives no mercy. Land the wrong way, jump the wrong way, and it could mean serious injury.

So when he had a real moment of "what am I doing with my life" on top of that platform, he was ridiculed. Sure, his body might have been physically ready, but that doesn't mean his head was on straight. I saw firsthand the panic and fear in his eyes when he was on top of that platform, questioning whether he was really ready to do it. If an athlete loses themselves in the air, it could have devastating consequences.

Why then, do we not uplift these athletes who are taking a pause and saying wait. Instead of diving back in feet first, he's stopping and thinking. That maybe he's more than just a diver. Diving is a sport of more than just physicality. Divers need to have awareness of every-thing around them. If they panic about what people might think about their dive, or if they aren't fully back, it can rock them to their core.

We don't focus on these athletes' mental health. Notable names have come out, long after they retired, and admitted that they shouldn't have played at times because they weren't all there, be it physically or mentally. We need more people to speak up while they're playing. No one should have to go into a game fearing the worst outcome all to please someone sitting on a couch in Anywhere, USA.

Athletes are more than their sport. Athletes are sons, daughters, husbands, and wives first. Athletes second. They owe nothing to anyone but themselves. Because long after the glory of their achieve-ments fade, and they step out of the limelight, and their name is no longer a household one, they are the only person they'll be with. And doesn't their opinion of themself hold more worth than anyone else's?

Instead of vilifying these athletes, we need to lift them up. To cheer when they say, 'I can't.' To celebrate them when they put their own mental health above sport. Because in this brave new world we live in, we all get the space to put ourselves first. And I for one will be cheering any athlete who does.

Chapter Twenty-Eight

FINN

"I'll admit, Finn. I'm impressed. I didn't think you had this in you."

I huff out a laugh. "I think there's a compliment somewhere in that insult."

"Can you blame me? My phone was ringing off the hook all week asking about the reporter who fell for his subject."

"It's not some cheap fling," I defend. "I know it's not professional, but we love each other, and whatever happens, we're in this together."

"Even if your job takes you out of the state?"

"What?"

Harry drops a stack of papers in front of me. "You've had offers coming in all morning from publications wanting to talk to you about joining their staff."

"You're kidding." Adjusting my glasses, I grab the stack and riffle through them. All of them are from big city papers, until the very last one.

Sports Weekly News.

The largest sports magazine in the country. Even not

knowing a thing about sports before this, I know of this magazine. It would be an incredible opportunity to write for them.

"Are you serious?"

Harry nods. "I'm sorry I ever doubted you, Anderson. This goes beyond just Wes. It's about every athlete who struggles and the way they are treated by fans. The feedback I've gotten on your article has been amazing. I'm proud of the work you put into this assignment."

I smooth a hand down my tie. "I was only thinking about Wes."

"Of course you were." He smirks at me. "So, have you given any thought as to what you want to do from here?"

"I came in here thinking I was going to be fired because I slept with my subject. Are you telling me I still have a future here?"

Harry nods back at me. "You can write your own ticket from here. I never thought I'd get something like this out of you. If I were you, I'd take the *Sports Weekly* position. At your age? It doesn't get any better than that."

"Isn't it in—"

"New York." Harry cuts off. "Again, you can write your own ticket from here. As much as I would love to keep you here, I know what an opportunity this is, and I don't want to stand in your way."

I stand, extending my hand to Harry. "I need some time to think about it. But I'll let you know what I decide."

"Of course. Don't take too long because these offers won't be around forever."

"Thanks, Harry."

"You did good, kid."

"*SPORTS WEEKLY NEWS* WANTS YOU?" Wes's jaw drops the moment I come in the house. I wasted no time leaving the office, wanting to get back home to Wes.

"Among other papers, yes." I gulp down the water in my hand, still not quite believing it.

"You have to take it."

"I don't have to do anything." Snark laces my voice. "Glad to know you want to get rid of me so quickly."

This is what I was worried about. That our paths would be too different and this relationship wouldn't be able to survive. Wes's entire career is here in Berkeley. Do I want to be with him? Yes. But would I be an idiot not to consider this opportunity? Also yes.

Wes stands, walking around the counter to stand in front of me. "If you think for a minute that I'm trying to get rid of you, you're out of your mind." He rests his hands on my chest, playing with the edges of my tie. "But I don't want to hold you back. This kind of opportunity doesn't come around often, which means you need to take it."

Grabbing his hands, I hold them to me. "I'm twenty-three years old. Who's to say another *better* opportunity won't come up in the future?"

"I just don't want to be the reason you hold yourself back."

I hate the pain in Wes's voice. The self-assured man I fell for is nowhere to be seen. I don't want to cause him any more pain, but it's hard to make him see what I truly want.

"Do you really think I could hold myself back if I'm with you on the road and bringing light to these kinds of issues? Maybe I can freelance for them and stay with the *Tribune*. We've got less than a year before the Olympics. After that, maybe I'll find another assignment that will be the dream."

"What if I don't go back to diving?" Wes's words are so quiet I almost miss them.

"Then you'll find something else that is your passion." Grasping his chin in my hand, I tilt his gaze to meet mine. Brown eyes filled with pain meet me. "I love you, Wes. And whether you decide to continue diving or decide to be a painter, I will be right by your side."

"A painter? Really?"

I nod, fighting back my smile. "I mean, you'd be terrible at it. But you'd have my full support."

"Sorry, I didn't mean to get so morose on you. We have a birthday party to go to."

"We can stay home." I hug Wes to me.

It's moments like this that I don't want to miss. Sure, the position with *Sports Weekly News* would be an amazing opportunity. But it doesn't hold a candle to being here with Wes.

I don't care where I write or who I write for. I only want to write articles that change the world. And this article might be the catalyst. If it means helping Wes and others like him, I'll do whatever, wherever, to help him.

"And miss a unicorn pool party? I've been looking forward to it all morning."

Chapter Twenty-Nine

FINN

"Hey! I didn't expect to see you guys," Melissa says, as she stacks presents on a table near the pool.

"I—" I start, but Wes cuts me off.

"We wouldn't have missed it."

He rubs my back, letting me know he's okay. I know I'm hovering. I can't help it. Ever since that day at the pool, I'm waiting for another panic attack. Whenever my sister had one, another would follow.

"Uncle Finn! Wes! Did you bring me a present?"

"Darcy. Don't be rude," my sister snaps. Darcy shrugs her shoulders and walks away. "Sorry."

"She's eight. It's fine, Melissa." I give her a kiss on the cheek and walk over to the food table, grabbing a handful of carrots.

"I don't think I've ever seen so many kids hopped up on sugar." Wes looks stunned as he stares around the busy pool. Kids are jumping in and out, shouting and running after each other.

"They seem pretty chill to me."

"This is chill?"

I nod my head. "I had to help my sister with a party last year and they had a movie party. Snacks on snacks on snacks. Made me realize I was okay being Uncle Finn."

"You really don't want kids?"

I don't even realize what I said until Wes says it back to me. "It's never been something I wanted. Not a conversation I expected to have today, but no. Do you?"

Wes's fingers link with mine, pulling me close to him. "No. With my training and traveling, it wouldn't be fair."

I let out a breath I don't realize I'm holding. "Glad we had that conversation."

"Yes. The stressed-out look on your face tells me you were very excited to have it."

The smile on Wes's face is the first genuine smile I've seen in days and it loosens the knot I'm carrying around in my chest.

"Uncle Finn! Will you play HORSE on the diving board with me?" Darcy appears at my side, tugging on my arm.

"Maybe in a little bit," I say, looking down at her big toothy grin.

"Would you settle for me?" Wes asks. My eyes fly to his, unsure if I heard him right.

"Do you know how to dive?"

Wes shakes his head from side to side. "A little."

"Okay." Darcy shrugs her shoulders and walks off toward the deep end of the pool.

"You know you don't have to do this, right?" Concern laces my voice. I still remember the haunted look in Wes's eyes when I helped him off that diving platform.

"You don't have to treat me with kid gloves, Finn. I'm fine playing a game with your niece. Besides, I've seen you dive."

He scurries out of my hold as I try to run after him. "Hey! I wasn't that bad!"

"I still want you to be the cool uncle. Besides, maybe Darcy will like her Uncle Wes."

It endears Wes even more to me that he wants to impress my niece. Even though we're still new, I know that Wes and I will be a family. And that we'll create our own family, whatever that looks like, together.

Together. I love how that word sounds. The smile on my face could be seen from the sun it's so bright as I find my place on the side of the pool to watch the competition. Darcy, the spunky kid that she is, is explaining the best way to dive to Wes.

"Why don't you go first and I'll follow you?" I can hear the playfulness in Wes's tone as Darcy gets on the diving board.

Darcy does an easy jump that Wes mimics without issue. The two of them keep going back and forth, Darcy giving Wes pointers every now and then.

"How about I try one first and you see if you can do it?" Wes asks, wiping the water out of his eyes.

"Okay!' Darcy is completely smitten with Wes as he makes his way to the end of the board. Looking over at me, he gives me a playful wink before launching off the board, doing a backward pike dive and splashing into the water.

"How? I mean, how?" Darcy is speechless as Wes pops up on the side of the pool, resting his chin on my knees.

"Darcy, you do know what Wes does, right?"

She shakes her head.

"I'm a diver." There's pride in Wes's voice.

"So you do that for a living?" The awe in Darcy's voice matches my own when I first watched Wes. It's hard for him not to win people over with his power and grace as he dives.

"I do."

"How do you learn? Can I learn?" Darcy is vibrating with eagerness.

"If it's okay with your mom, I can show you a few things."

"Yes!" She pumps her fist and then runs off, shouting for her mom.

"Look at you." I lean back on my hands, watching Wes as he still floats in the water.

"What? If she wants to learn, I can teach her." He brushes it off like it's no big deal.

"Hey, Finn. I could use some help," Melissa calls over to me.

"Don't think we're done talking about this." I drop a kiss on Wes's wet lips and head toward my sister, wondering what kind of turn this day just took.

WES

THE CRACKLING warmth from the firepit glows in the late summer night. It's dark, the fog from the city blocking the normal stunning view.

"Beer?" Finn hands me a drink as he takes a seat next to me. I take it from him, gulping down a sip.

"Thanks."

Finn extends his free hand to me. I take it without hesitation. I love this man, getting to touch him in any way I can.

"So you seemed pretty okay volunteering to teach Darcy how to dive."

I let out a deep breath, releasing everything I've been carrying on my shoulders these last few weeks.

"To be honest? It was the first time in a long time where I felt like I was going to be okay."

"Really?"

I take a sip of my beer, setting it on the edge of the firepit. Standing, I move to sit on Finn's lap. "Really. I realize now how limited my vision for the future was. It was only training and competitions and nothing else. I've never thought far enough ahead of what I'm going to do after diving and I think that's why everything has been piling up."

"But then you got injured and all of a sudden the end was closer than ever before."

I stroke his strong jaw, loving how I don't need to explain it to him.

"Yes. I haven't given it a second thought, and then Darcy asked me to show her a thing or two. And I realized why can't I do that? Be a coach when it's time to hang up my Speedo?"

Finn's fingers find the hair at the back of my neck, tugging me down to meet his waiting lips. It feels new, but familiar. Too short, but I know we'll have forever to do this.

"You would be an incredible coach, Wes."

"You really think so?"

"I know it. You've been there. You know what it takes to compete at all levels. I hate that you know what it's like to come back from an injury, but you have real life experience that people would kill to learn from."

Finn is oozing excitement.

"And I could coach anywhere."

Now he looks confused. "Why wouldn't you coach here?"

I brush a stray lock of hair off Finn's forehead. The fire reflects in his glasses, hiding his eyes from me. "You've already gotten one offer from a huge magazine. When you become this big-time journalist, people from all over the world will want you to write for them. What if you get the opportunity to go to Washington? Or London?"

"And what if the opportunity I want is right here in Berkeley?"

"I don't want you passing up an opportunity because of me."

"Wes." Finn shakes his head. "The news world is changing. I can travel to where the news is. But Harry is letting me write my own ticket now. So what if I want to stick with you and write your story until the Olympics?"

My heart feels like it might burst out of my chest. "You really want to do that? You'd give up the opportunity to write for *Sports Weekly News* to be here with me?"

"I love you, Wes. But I wouldn't be giving anything up. Your story is worth telling. You inspire so many people, and I want my words to be the words to do the inspiring. Your journey is special, and I don't want anyone else getting to tell it but me."

"I fucking love you." Our lips crash together in the most epic kiss I've ever been a part of it. It's soft and powerful, and I feel the ground shift beneath me. It's no longer just me floating through life on my own. It's me and Finn.

"Wes." The need in Finn's voice settles in my groin and has me hardening. We haven't been together since before I had my panic attack at the dive center. My body aches for his in a way I've never felt.

I stand, pulling Finn up with me. The gleam in his eyes

ignites the fire in me. Walking into the house, Finn crowds behind me, his lips finding my neck. "I've missed you, Wes."

"I've always been right here." I wrap his arms around my waist, leading us into my room.

"But you've been in pain. And I would do anything I could to take it away."

I spin, sitting down on my bed and pulling Finn between my legs. "You've been here for me in every way imaginable, Finn. I wouldn't be where I am right now if it weren't for you."

"There is nowhere else I'd rather be."

No more words need to be said. We both strip down, baring our naked souls to one another. The tender way we touch one another brings a piece of me back to myself.

As I slide into Finn, I know it's home. He is home. That no matter what happens, no matter what my future might bring, I'll have this man by my side. And I'll be by his side.

And there's no other place I'd rather be.

Chapter Thirty

"How are you feeling today? Are you sure you're ready for this?"

Thank God, Finn still has special access, because he's with me in the locker rooms. It's the first major competition since my meltdown—the first Olympic qualifying event for the games this summer.

Resting my hands on Finn's shoulders, I pierce him with my most confident stare. "I'm fine. I promise. I got this."

Finn blows out a breath, his gaze taking in everything around him. He's been antsy all week. I know my first major competition has been hard on him. Finn has been watching my every move, just waiting to see if I'll break down. But after taking some time off, I know I have it in me to do this.

I'm steady.

I'm calm.

I'm ready.

Every dive I've been making has been building my confidence. And every day I come home to Finn. Life has become so much more than diving. And that alone has let me focus on the sport I love.

"Sorry. I know you do. Is it bad I'm more nervous than you?"

I bring Finn in for a kiss. "No. And I love you for it. But I'm good. I got this."

Patting his arms, I back away, heading toward the pool deck.

"I'll see you when I'm done. I'll be the one wearing the gold medal."

Finn rolls his eyes but follows me, taking his usual seat in the stands with my mom. Everyone from the team is crowding around the team area, the NorCal team starting their warm-up dives.

"Is everyone clear on the diving order? Wes, you're up first." Damien shifts his gaze to me. "You good with that?"

"Would everyone relax? I'm fine."

"It's okay if you're nervous," Damien says, trying to get more out of me.

"I'm not. If I was having any problems, I would tell you."

"Then let's get this show on the road."

I rub my hands together, eager to start diving. I've been anxious for this moment. It's been building for the last few months, and I'm eager for my first major international competition. I've been itching for it. I'm sure I've made Finn crazy, but now that it's finally here, I know I've got this.

My first dive is one I've been doing for years. It's one I'm comfortable with, that I could perform in my sleep. The inward three-and-a-half somersaults is also one of my favorites.

Loosening up my arms, I hear my name over the loud-speaker and start the trek up the platform. I've done dives from up here thousands of times. It's hard not to remember the one time I failed while up here. But as I hit the top deck, I wipe everything from my mind. The smell of chlorine and the hard concrete beneath my feet is what I focus on.

Taking a deep breath, I walk to the edge of the platform. The height has never bothered me. Picking a spot, I push off, spinning and somersaulting before straightening my body as I glide into the pool. Exploding out of the water, I can't wipe the grin off my face.

The dive felt incredible. The power moving through my body is something I haven't felt in a long time. It felt good. The cheers from the crowd are electric.

I hit the shower at the base of the tower after I get out of the pool and make my way over to the team.

"Wes. That was incredible." Damien slaps a hand on my back as I wipe a towel over my body.

"It felt good."

"Good? I don't think I've ever seen you dive like that."

I smile, shaking my head at Damien's praise. Praise that is warranted when my top scores hit the board.

"Okay, that was better than good." I laugh, taking a minute to bask in my scores. Never have I gotten a first score that good.

"You keep doing that and you could qualify for the Olympics this weekend."

Clasping my hands behind my head, I let out a breath I didn't realize I was holding. "Okay, Damien. Let's not get ahead of ourselves."

The rest of the dives for the afternoon go much of the same way. But it's not only me. Both Simone and Dan have had a really great day. We're all at the top of our game today, which propels us into the top for the finals tomorrow.

And yet, it's not even the best part of my day. That's reserved for Finn. Because of the team debrief, I meet him at the hotel. Pushing the door open to our room—a perk of him now traveling with me is staying together—I'm met with the biggest grin.

"You did it!" Finn rushes me, smothering me in a hug.

"It was day one of qualifiers. Finals are tomorrow."

"I don't care. Do you realize how well you did? You scored almost six hundred points. That's incredible." Finn pulls back, attacking my lips with his. A chuckle escapes me.

"What are you laughing at?" Finn pulls back, giving me a glare.

"Just remembering the first time you showed up at practice. Telling me you gave my dive a ten out of ten." I wrap my arms around his shoulders, pulling him in close. Just where I like him. "And now here you are knowing how to score my dives."

A smile plays across his lips. "Well, I had a good teacher."

I back Finn farther into the room, his knees hitting the bed as he collapses on top of it. My fingers find his hair, relishing the feel beneath me. "Maybe I can teach you another thing or two."

Finn shakes his head. "No. Absolutely not. Keep it in your pants, Cooper."

"Wow, okay." I drop my hands, taking a step back from him.

"I have an ice bath all drawn up for you. You need to rest. I saw how you performed today, and you'll need all the recovery time you can get if you're going to do that again tomorrow."

Finn stands, grabbing my hand and taking me into the bathroom. "And they say romance is dead."

"True love." Finn hooks a finger in my sweats, pulling me closer toward him. "Now strip."

Pushing my pants and boxers down, I whip my shirt over my head. "Usually this has much better results."

"Yeah, yeah. Put these on so you don't freeze, and maybe if you're good, I'll let you snuggle before bed."

Putting on the swim trunks Finn hands me, I dip into the icy water in the bathtub. My breath escapes me as the water hits my skin. Goosebumps break out all over my body. I hate ice baths, but I can't deny the benefits.

Finn sits on the toilet, crossing his long legs in front of him. "How ya feelin'?"

"As much as I hate it, thank you." I drop my head against the tile. "You don't have to stay in here with me."

Finn waves me off. "I've already written my article and submitted it. There's nowhere else I'd rather be."

"We're in Montreal. You didn't want to go and see the sights?"

A warm hand closes around mine. "The only sights I want to see are right here."

Warmth slides over me, counteracting the cold of the ice. "I owe you a nice vacation when the season is over."

"Paris?" Finn can't hide the excitement in his voice.

"Whatever you want, Finn. You deserve it."

"Hey." Finn squeezes my hand, bringing my attention to him. "We both do. It's been a crazy year for both of us. Once the season is over, you and me. Top of the Eiffel Tower. Drinking Champagne. That's something they do, right?"

I link my fingers with Finn's, drawing his hand to my lips and dropping a kiss on his knuckles. "Champagne. Macarons. And kissing. Don't forget about the kissing."

Finn gets up, kneeling next to me, running a hand

through my hair. I lean into his touch. "What's got you feeling all lovey today?"

His blue eyes meet mine. "Today was a good day. I don't think anyone thought I could do it. But I did. And even though it felt incredible, it wasn't the best part of my day."

"And what was?"

"Coming back here to you. Knowing that even if I screwed up and I don't qualify this weekend, it wouldn't be the end of the world. Do you know what that feels like?"

Finn shakes his head.

"For once I don't feel the pressure, like winning is the only thing that matters. Because it's not the be all, end all for me anymore."

"And what is?"

"You."

Epilogue

FINN - SIX MONTHS LATER

"I think you're more nervous than Wes," Mary chirps in my ear.

It's been a long year. Endless training, early mornings and earlier nights, sacrifices made. But it all comes down to this. Wes's final dive in the Olympics.

With my article gaining national attention last summer, I've been freelancing more for major publications. It's the best of both worlds—writing what I love, articles of substance, while also chronicling Wes's journey to this point. My fingers are itching to write the story of him winning gold.

He's in second place, sitting a few points behind the best diver in the world. Silver would be amazing, but I want gold. He deserves gold.

It certainly wasn't the easiest road back here for Wes. He wasn't sure if he could come back after his injury, after his breakdown, but his diving has never been better. He was able to come back stronger because of the support system he built. Me. His family. His teammates who have become family.

"I just know how hard he's been training for this. I want it for him more than anything." It's so close, I can almost taste it.

"And yet, if he doesn't get it, he'll still come home to a loving husband and have a good life."

I smile at Mary. Wes and I got married this past spring in a small ceremony with close friends and family. We didn't care that we'd only been together for nine months.

And it was the perfect day—followed by an even more perfect long weekend in Paris. It's been nothing short of perfect days, because no matter what happens, we both come home to each other.

Wes starts walking up the platform, and my nerves grow with each step he takes. This dive is a four point one, the highest degree of difficulty out of any dive at this Olympics, even higher than the current person sitting in first.

As he steps to the edge of the platform, I take a deep breath, holding Mary's hand tight in my own. The four and a half somersaults with a twist at the end has been something he's been perfecting for months now. And he has one final shot to nail it for gold.

WES

IT'S BEEN a long road to get here. After my break from the sport, I came back feeling better than ever. Having Finn at my side makes any challenge I face that much easier. Because I'm not just a diver. I'm a husband and a son. An uncle and a friend.

So standing here at the edge of the platform, I know no matter what happens, I'll be going home a winner.

Taking one last breath, the echoes of the aquatic center are drowned out as I push off the board, spinning and twisting before throwing my arms up and gliding into the water.

It was the perfect dive. I know it the second I come up, and it's evident in the smile on my face. The crowd is raucous. I swim over, climbing out of the pool as Damien makes his way over to me.

"Brilliant, Wes! You crushed it!" He wraps me in a hug as I await my score.

"It felt amazing." I keep my arm wrapped around his shoulders as the scores come in. Tens across the board. A perfect dive, catapulting me into first place with one diver left.

"Yes!" I pump my fists before crushing Damien in a hug.

"You did it! I am so fucking proud of you!" he shouts in my ear.

My nerves start swarming as the last diver, arguably the best in the world, steps onto the platform and gives a performance worthy of gold.

My eyes are drawn to the scoreboard, waiting for the final score. Damien clutches my hand in his, squeezing for dear life. It feels like hours before the scores are finally splashed across the big screen. Ten. Ten. Nine point five. Second place.

"Holy shit. Holy shit!" I cover my face as tears start to pour down my face.

"You did it!" Damien is slapping my back, yelling in my ear as the crowd starts chanting my name. "Gold!"

I stand up, waving my hands in the air to the crowd, and it's then that I see Finn. He's screaming his head off, giving everyone around him high fives. But when he locks eyes with me, I race over to the stands.

He's down there in a second, extending his hand as far as it can go, and I grasp it, holding on with everything I have. He's crying just as hard as I am.

"You did it, Wes." Nothing else needs to be said. So much love is pouring out of Finn and it makes this moment all the more special that I get to share it with him.

"Go get that gold." He squeezes my hand as I pull away from him, blowing kisses to him and my mom.

"We love you, Wes!" she shouts from behind Finn. I wave to her and then head back to the deck, everyone swarming me to offer their congratulations.

"Great job!"

"Best dive I've ever seen."

"If I had to lose, I'm glad it was to you."

My head is swimming in the best way. Finding my gear, I head back toward the locker rooms to change for the medal ceremony.

It's all a whirlwind. But the moment I step onto the podium, I can finally absorb what's happening around me.

From the moment of breakdown last year to now, I never thought I'd be here—accepting diving's highest honor on the world's biggest stage. It's been a long road back. And I can't believe I made it. As the gold medal is draped around my neck, the weight of it is more than just my road back.

It's the fact that I'm an out athlete celebrating. That my husband is here with me to share in this moment. The national anthem playing means so much more than just representing my country.

"How are you feeling, Wes? What does this moment mean to you?" a reporter asks after the ceremony, shoving a mic in my face. Everything is a blur, and it's all a bit surreal.

"It's hard to believe this is happening. I've dreamed about this moment my entire life, and now that it's here, it's hard to put into words." My voice breaks. It's hard to keep my emotions in check right now.

"Did you think you'd get here after coming back from your injury?"

My eyes search the stands, trying to find Finn. "If it wasn't for my husband, I don't think I would have. He has been the biggest support system I have. If it weren't for him, I might've quit. But he kept me going on the hard days. And there were a lot of hard days mixed in with the good."

"Wes, congratulations. Go enjoy this moment."

The reporter dismisses me, and leaving the pool deck, I make my way to the family and friends area. All I can think about is getting to Finn. Adrenaline is still pulsing through me as I spot him through the hordes of people. He doesn't waste a second, running over to me and jumping into my arms.

"You did it!" I'm holding on as tight as he is, his tears soaking through my team jacket.

"I couldn't have done it without you," I manage to choke out. "I can't believe I did it."

Finn drops his legs, pulling back to look at me. His strong hands cup my cheeks. "Wes. There is no one more deserving than you. You were incredible."

I pull him to me, clinging to him as the tears come again. I've never been more emotional about a win. This is everything I've worked for, and I can't believe I get to share it with Finn.

Another hand comes down on my arm. "Have time to give your mom a hug?"

Wiping my eyes, I pull away from him and wrap her petite frame in my arms. "I'm so proud of you. My sweet boy is an Olympic champion."

"Geez, Mom. You're going to make me cry," I laugh.

"Oh, like you weren't crying before." She pulls back, wiping her eyes.

Finn wraps an arm around my shoulder, pulling me into his side. "No, no tears here. None at all."

"If it weren't for you two, I'd be fine." I rest my hand on Finn's chest, trying to catch my breath and calm my racing heart.

After everything that we've been through, it's hard to believe this moment is here. That Finn is here with me. He saw me at my lowest and didn't flinch. Finn was there for me every step of the way.

"How are you feeling?" Finn whispers in my ear.

I shut my eyes, committing everything about this to memory. It's a day I won't ever forgot, but this is the best part, right here. Being wrapped up in my husband's arms and sharing this with him. I could've come in dead last, and I'd still be happy. Because I have Finn.

"Like I won gold."

The End

Read on to find out all about Wes and Finn's honeymoon!

Bonus Epilogue

WES

"**L**ooks like we're both wrong."

"You're surprised it doesn't look like a hairy cock and balls or a rocket ship?" Finn questions. We're standing at the base of the Eiffel Tower. Metal beams stretch out into the sky above us.

I laugh. "Thank God we were both wrong. Is it everything you wanted?"

"It's better than I imagined." Wrapping an arm around Finn, he sinks into my hold. Paris is beautiful in the springtime. And what better time than that to finally take our honeymoon.

With the Olympics coming this summer, I didn't want to wait to marry Finn. With his support, I've been able to return to the sport I love and be able to compete at the highest level. Without him, I don't know where I'd be. So, after one particularly grueling training session, I suggested we get married. And even though it'd only been a few months, Finn jumped into my arms with a resounding 'yes!'

With nonstop training, we found the only free day we

could find in our busy schedule. Finn and I planned a small ceremony with our closest friends and family, nothing over the top. We wanted it to be just the two of us finally joining our lives together. And now, a mere few months before the games, we're taking some much needed rest together.

Ever since Finn's article ran, he's been asked to free-lance more and more pieces on athletes in various sports. All while traveling the world with me and documenting my return to the Olympics. He's in high demand, but even so, he's still at my side. I couldn't be prouder of the work he's doing.

And after the craziness of the Olympics this summer, he'll be helping me write my own story. My journey has been well documented, but Finn has inspired me to tell it in my words. Not his or anyone else's.

"Thank you for bringing me here." Finn spins around in my arms, the early evening lights reflecting off his glasses. "I'm so glad we found the time to come."

I drop my forehead to his. "I'll always make the time for you, Finn."

He steals a kiss, the Eiffel Tower now lighting up behind us. "I love you."

I sigh, further wrapping my arms around him. "You know, I've never actually seen the Eiffel Tower like this."

"You haven't?"

"No. The only time I came here was for a competition. We were in and out before I had time to enjoy anything more than room service."

Finn moves in front of me, his hands taking mine. "I'm glad we get to experience this together."

Stepping back into the swarm of people, Finn walks us down by the river, linking hands and strolling into the Paris night, the city lit up in front of us. I don't think I could have imagined a more perfect time here. If only we had more time.

"Do you know I pictured this once?"

"You did?"

I stop Finn, spinning him to rest against the stone wall that lines the river below. "When we painted those God-awful pictures of the Eiffel Tower." Finn laughs, those terrible paintings still hanging, ruined, in our dining room.

"I imagined us walking down the Seine just like this." I drop my eyes to our joined hands, bringing them to my lips, pressing a kiss to each knuckle. "I wanted so badly to be the one to bring you here. You talked about wanting to visit, and I wanted it to be me who brought you here."

"And would you look at that?" Pulling a hand out of my grasp, Finn wiggles the shiny band adorning his ring finger. I love seeing it there. "You brought your husband."

I stare deep into Finn's eyes. Eyes that I will never grow tired of looking into. "I still remember that day. That feeling I had. It was a physical ache, wanting to be with you here. I knew at that moment that you were the one for me."

"Really? That was like our, what, second date?" Finn tugs me closer to him, our chests brushing together.

I nod. "And I knew it then. When you came into my life that day at the pool, I knew my life had changed. Didn't know how, but I did."

Finn traces a finger over my lips, as if he'll forget the shape of them. "I never told you my first impression of you, did I?"

I shake my head.

"It was like Baywatch."

"Stop it." I shove off him, spinning on my heel back into the busy sidewalk.

"I'm serious." Finn grabs my hand, pulling me back to

him and anchoring me to him. "You were getting out of the pool and I don't think I've ever been more mesmerized by a person before. Without a doubt, you were the sexiest man I've ever seen."

"I feel like you're trying to tell me I'm a dumb jock or something." I laugh, but I want to hear more. I could listen to Finn tell me stories all day.

Finn's brows furrow in annoyance. "If you'd let me finish…"

I bring my hands up in surrender.

"Thank you." Finn grabs my hands and pulls them into his chest, resting over his heart. "You were the sexiest man I'd ever seen that day. But what I came to learn about you put everything else to shame. You're kind. And driven. And have so much love to give, that some days I don't feel worthy of it. And the fact that you chose me? I'm lucky beyond my wildest dreams."

"Do you remember what else I remember about that date?" There's a quiver to my voice, my emotions betraying me."

"What about it?" Finn squeezes my hand, the gentle reminder that it's okay to be vulnerable with him.

"Do you remember what I said the French were known for?"

A smile so bright that it could bring me to my knees lights up Finn's face. "Kissing."

"You remember."

Finn scoffs. "Talk of kissing you? That's hard to forget."

"The instructor was so mad at us and I remember kissing you and having paint all over our faces."

A laugh bursts out of his chest. "She hated us."

"She really did. But that is still one of my favorite nights. Being with you."

Finn wraps his arms around me, his hands drifting under my coat and warming me all over.

"Then how about a little less talk, and a little more kissing?"

And just like that, I seal my lips to his.

Just me and the man I love in the City of Lights.

No more talking needed.

Want to read about Wes and Finn's wedding?
Then scan the QR code below and grab it now!

Author's Note

Book number 8 is out in the world!

It's hard to believe that in the last 17 months I have written 7 full length books and co-written another! It's been a hard 17 months, but I wouldn't trade it for the world! I have met some of the most amazing people that have become dear friends and have the absolute best readers in the world!

This book was born out of a love for the Olympic Games and watching Simone Biles take a step back during the games. The courage it must have taken her to do that inspired me, and was a big part of why I decided to write this story.

Thank you to Menotah, my amazing beta reader for helping me make this book what it is! Thank you to all of my author friends, who are too many to name. I don't know where I would be without all of you! And to my Street Team…thank you for loving my books and giving me the push to keep writing.

To all the readers and bloggers who read my books and share the love…I wouldn't be anywhere without you!

About the Author

After winning a Young Author's Award in second grade, Emily Silver was destined to be a writer. She loves writing strong heroines and the swoony men who fall for them.

A lover of all things romance, Emily started writing books set in her favorite places around the world. As an avid traveler, she's been to all seven continents and sailed around the globe.

When she's not writing, Emily can be found sipping cocktails on her porch, reading all the romance she can get her hands on and planning her next big adventure!

Find her on social media to stay up to date on all her adventures and upcoming releases!

The Denver Mountain Lions

Roughing The Kicker

Pass Interference

Sideline Infraction

Illegal Contact

The Big Game

Dixon Creek Ranch

Yours To Lose - newsletter bonus story

Yours to Take - coming March 23, 2023

Yours to Hold - coming June 29, 2023

Yours to Be - coming August 24, 2023

Yours to Forget - coming November 16, 2023

Off the Deep End — A standalone, MM sports romance

The Ainsworth Royals

Royal Reckoning

Reckless Royal

Royal Relations

Royal Roots

Royal Ties

The Love Abroad Series

An Icy Infatuation

A French Fling

A Sydney Surprise

Get all my titles now: